Between the Levees

Jonathan Olivier

Aunt Leola

Thank you for reading
my debut novel. I hope you
enjoy it!.

Jonathan Olivier

Between the Levees

Printed in the United States of America

Editor: Tiffany Dawn Munn
Copy Editor: Rachel Blackbirdsong
Cover Design: Charlie Th'ng

First printing, 2016

ISBN 978-0-9977318-0-4

JonathanOlivier.com

To my mother, Belinda.
Her guidance and support made this work possible.

One

It wasn't much of a clue—just the name of a man, Vincent Dupuis (Doo-pwee), and the small village in southern Louisiana called Bayou Pigeon where he supposedly lived. But it was a lead, and Sam couldn't argue with that, especially after the dead end he'd hit in the weeks before.

Sam climbed into his white rental car, covered in a layer of dew that hadn't yet evaporated thanks to the morning humidity. He turned the key in the ignition, beginning another hour-long drive to the tiny Cajun settlement that was a straight shot to the south from his hotel. It was a muggy morning in late August, his third day in Louisiana, and just as hot as the two previous ones had been. The days of commuting hadn't been wasted, though, and neither would this one since it gave him much-needed time to reflect.

What little Sam knew about Vincent was from court documents dating back to 1988, which revealed that Vincent had, for some reason, petitioned the state of Louisiana to gain custody of him after his parents died. But getting in touch with the man to find out why was proving next to impossible. Vincent's only contact information from the courthouse was ambiguously listed as "Bayou Pigeon," leaving

Sam with only the option of going door-to-door to inquire if anyone in the village knew the man. So far, Vincent's identity still eluded him.

It was starting to appear as if Vincent was a ghost, some specter from the past that no one quite remembered.

Sam shook his head with a wry smile. It would be just his luck that his search for information about his parents would lead him, not to answers, but more questions that he might never be able to resolve. His bout of bad luck made him wonder if he was headed toward another dead end.

As his car rattled over the poorly maintained road, he thought of his parents, Ryan and Martha Landry. They had been dead for years, practically all his life, and he knew virtually nothing about them. Not that he hadn't tried to learn more over the years. Nathan and Evelyn Miller, distant relatives who gained custody of him and moved him to Boston as a child, didn't have anything to tell him on the subject. Sam only uncovered that they weren't his real parents shortly before his teenage years, when Evelyn was deteriorating from cancer. After her death, Nathan became aloof, detached, and abusive, even discouraging Sam from wanting to find answers about his parents. And he did a good job of it. He'd say, "What's the point? They're dead, just like Evelyn. You've got what you've got. Learn to live with it." So that's what Sam did, and he gave up on finding answers. He never tried to discover anything, even after striking out on his own at seventeen. It took eight years before his lonely, stagnant life became too much for him. After a night of coming too close to hitting the bottle—something he vowed he'd never again do—he knew he needed to find out who his family was. He knew that he needed to uncover who he was, too.

Sam's mind was thrust back to the battered road as his car slammed into another pothole he'd failed to see. They lined the roads around Bayou Pigeon every few feet. Patches of asphalt, which were meant to mend the dangerous holes along the black top, acted more as speed bumps that violently jolted his vehicle if hit at the wrong angle. He should've learned his lesson the days before, but his wandering mind made it difficult to focus. The diminutive sedan he rented from the airport didn't make navigating the harsh roads any easier.

The roads seemed to be indicative of the general aura that surrounded the places he drove past. Buildings were old and decrepit, many of them containing green mold stains on the exterior walls. A majority of the structures were mobile homes, placed here and there between stretches of water and trees, hardly ever clustering in more than groups of five. Some of the lawns could barely be considered so, as the homes were surrounded by stained swamp water on almost every side. Virtually all of the trailers sat atop cinder blocks to keep the occupants dry, and most of the homeowners had multiple boats, often three or four, stashed in the front yard.

Despite the mold-riddled trailers dotting most of the area, Sam also rode past a few stately houses with fresh primped lawns. He thought the homes looked out of place, with a backdrop of dense trees and undergrowth just beyond the cookie cutter properties. They were fewer in number than the mobile homes, and spaced farther apart, but were present every so often on high ground—prime real estate in the swampy lowlands. These dwellings, like the trailers, were often raised above the ground with at least a boat or two stored in the front yard.

Sam looked in the rear view mirror for a routine check of his surroundings, but there was no one behind him. No real surprise there. His baby blue eyes popped brightly compared to the car's drab-gray interior that filled the sides of the mirror. He had a thin, yet athletic frame that stopped just shy of six feet. His rounded face gave him a youthful look, and his inability to grow much facial hair knocked a few more years off his appearance, making him look younger than twenty-five.

The buildings began to cluster closer together, and Sam realized he was nearing the village. His GPS emitted one final command, instructing him to turn right onto Bayou Pigeon Road, which would take him near the center of the village. He pushed the rolled-up sleeves of his white button-down shirt farther up his arms. Sweat dribbled down his chest and made his shirt cling to him. He knew it'd be hot that time of year, but he wasn't fully prepared for the onslaught of the notorious Louisiana humidity. Cranking the air conditioner on high with the windows up would have alleviated much of the oppressive heat, but he felt the need for fresh air to keep him calm. With the window rolled down, his long, blonde hair settled as he slowed the car. The front of his hair was styled neatly with a band that wrapped around his head and was positioned just behind his ears, a style he employed on most days. His locks had a slight curl to them, and hung down almost to his shoulders.

He turned right off the crude road and onto another that had seen equivalent under-maintenance. He motored the car across a two-lane bridge with a subtle arch, over what he thought to be the namesake bayou of the village. On his first day, he wasn't sure he was even in the right place. There were no signs designating Bayou Pigeon and no discernable downtown or town square. Only three or four connecting roads with the occasional business and house comprised the entire place. The tiny fishing village was simply a dot of humanity in an immense swath of swamp.

Sam thought the sheer minute size of the village would give him an advantage, as he figured a place so small would surely have residents that knew most everyone. But his conversations the two days before with locals at a fire station, a hole-in-the-wall library, and a few random homes resulted in nothing. He was trying to stay optimistic, but the heat—and the mosquitoes—were making it difficult.

He pulled off to the side of the road, inching into the parking lot of a gas station. Only two gas pumps were available and they both appeared to not be in working order. He shifted the car into park and looked around to make sure the place wasn't abandoned. A late '90s model Chevy truck parked next to a school-bus-yellow sedan not far from the building was a promising sign that the place was open for business.

"Here goes day three," he said, looking toward the convenience store. He took a few deep breaths to ready himself and trudged across the parking lot toward the building, perspiring just in the twenty or so steps needed to reach the entrance. He pushed open a glass door, causing a dinky bell to ring, which alerted the cashier to his presence. She was a heavy-set lady and had dark brown hair in a drooping bun. Her soiled T-shirt did nothing to compliment her green eyes hidden behind thick glasses.

"How you doing today, hun?" she said in a welcoming manner with a Cajun twang.

Her warm welcome surprised Sam, but it made it easier to strike up a conversation. "I'm doing well, and yourself?"

"Certainly can't complain. Can I help you with something?"

"I'm looking for someone, actually."

"Well, I'll do my best to help you out," she said, perking up with alertness.

"I'm looking for a man named Vincent Dupuis. I'm not even sure if he lives around here anymore but does that name happen to ring a bell?"

She raised her eyebrows and rubbed her chin. Then she shook her head and gave Sam an all too familiar response. "No, honey, I'm sorry but it sure don't. I know a few Dupuis that live around here, but no Vincent I can think of. I can get you a phone book to look through if you want."

"I guess it couldn't hurt."

Sam peered over the dimly lit interior of the building while the cashier fumbled under the cabinet. The inside of the store fared no better than the outside. While there was no mold, brown paneling that looked older than he was graced the walls. Only three aisles of snack food and canned goods were available for perusing customers. Toward the back of the room, an old man sat next to a counter that housed a coffee pot and a few foam cups, nestled between an assortment of sugar and creamers.

"Here you go," she said as she handed him a small, local phone book more than a decade old.

"Thanks." He flipped through the pages and scanned the list of names. Sliding his finger carefully down the list of Cajun surnames he could barely pronounce, he found two people bearing the Dupuis last name, but no Vincent.

"You find it, honey?" she asked as Sam flipped the book closed.

He handed it back to her. "Sure didn't."

"Well, I wish I could help you out more. I'm sorry."

"No need for apologies. Thank you for your help," he said with a smile.

He walked out the door of the convenience store and stood near the entrance to gather his thoughts. The little enthusiasm he first had took a blow, replaced by the nervousness that had steadily grown throughout the entirety of the journey. He was starting to think Vincent might not be alive or had left the area. Regardless, he wasn't about to give up; he had come too far. Even though he was leaving for Boston the next afternoon, he shook off any negative thoughts—he still had plenty of daylight to continue looking.

He headed for the rental car while still trying to devise a better plan of where to look next. Before he could grasp the door handle, he heard the voice of the cashier. He looked back as she called him from the front of the store, waving her hands in the air. Sam's eyes widened as he turned back toward her.

"I'm glad I caught you 'fore you left," she said, half her body extending out of the doorway to prop the glass door open. "Come inside, there's a fella in here who overheard you talking. Says he might know who you talking about."

Sam didn't utter a word, but just nodded his head. His body instinctively moved him toward the friendly stranger and back into the dingy convenience store. She motioned him to follow her inside, down one of the thin aisles to where the coffee was housed. When they neared the counter topped with the coffee pot, she pointed to the old man Sam had seen a few moments earlier.

"His name is Mr. Lloyd," she said to Sam. "Here's the young man you over heard, Mr. Lloyd. He's, well, I don't even know his name. I'm Betsy." She held her hand to her chest and smiled.

"I'm Sam Miller. Thanks for all your help."

Walking back to tend the register, Betsy smiled again. "Oh, honey, it ain't nothing. You're welcome."

Sam focused his attention to Lloyd. "Hello," he said, extending his hand out. "I'm Sam. It's nice to meet you."

Lloyd's aged, right hand stretched out and met Sam's, while his other gripped firmly on an orange coffee mug. Sam thought it looked as if Lloyd hadn't changed clothes since the '70s. They weren't dirty as much as they were aged. A blue and green striped shirt accentuated with beige suspenders was tucked into faded, blue jeans with baseball-sized rips at both knees. The high-seated, retro trucker cap and square-frame bifocals completed the dated getup.

"You looking for Vincent, huh?" the old man said after shaking Sam's hand then taking a swig of coffee.

The strong Cajun accent was hard for Sam to understand, but he did his best to decipher it. "I sure am. Do you know where I can find him?"

"Yeah, I do. But what you want with ole Vin? I'm surprised a young fella like you even knows who he is."

"Why's that?"

"Vin is probably 50 or 60 years older than you I would have to guess. And he likes to keep to himself."

Sam raised his eyebrows, a bit surprised to find out Vincent was so much his senior. "Well, Lloyd, I suppose you could say he's a friend."

Wrinkles formed around Lloyd's eyes as he peered at Sam through his wide glasses. "You not a cop or nothing, huh?" Lloyd said with curiosity.

Sam thought Lloyd's apprehension was a bit odd, and the question made him slow to respond. "Nope, not a cop."

Lloyd laughed. "I didn't think so. But you never know these days." He took another slurp of coffee and smiled. "Vin's a friend of mine."

Finally, Sam thought, someone who could confirm Vincent's whereabouts. He quickly responded. "Really? Could you tell me how to find him?"

The old Cajun looked Sam up and down, as if he was attempting to understand what Sam wanted with Vincent. "I don't mean to be asking too many questions. It's just when an out of towner comes looking for a man that hardly anyone even knows around here, it makes me a little curious."

Sam didn't know how to explain to Lloyd what he wanted with Vincent other than with the truth. "He knew my parents and I'm just trying to track him down."

"No kidding. Who's your parents?"

"Ryan and Martha Landry. Did you know them?" Sam said excitedly as his eyes widened.

Lloyd shook his head. "I don't think so."

Sam's smile faded and he looked toward the floor.

Lloyd must have noticed the topic held quite a bit of importance with Sam, because then he stood from his chair and, with the aid of a wooden cane, walked a few steps toward the entrance of the store. "It ain't that hard to get there. Shouldn't take you all that long, either."

Sam followed with renewed hope as Lloyd gave him directions.

"When you turn outta here, take a left, then go all the way down the road for about ten minutes," the old Cajun instructed, pointing in the direction that Sam needed to drive. "You gonna hit gravel and then another ten minutes down there, a little road veers off from the levee on the left and tucks into the woods. His house is a little ways down a dirt road."

Sam smiled and nodded. "And that's it?"

"That's it. If he's home, his ole, blue Ford truck will be parked out in front his house."

"Seems easy enough," Sam said, bidding Lloyd farewell with a handshake. "Thank you, I appreciate the help."

"Tell him Lloyd sent you. He don't have too many surprise visitors. He may think you a tax collector or something."

"As long as he doesn't think I'm a cop," Sam said, which sparked a round of laughter from Lloyd.

"It was nice to meet you, Sam," Lloyd said through a few lingering laughs. He took his seat back near the coffee pot and waved. "You have a good day."

"Thanks," Sam said. For the first time since he arrived, it looked like he finally would.

Two

Sam spotted a crude driveway nestled between rows of cattails just as he zoomed past it. He slammed on the car's brakes, causing the small vehicle to slide across the gravel and whip up dirt that billowed over the hood and windshield. Homes and businesses completely disappeared by this point, and all he was surrounded by were trees to his left and the levee, a manmade hill to halt flood water, to his right.

When the dust settled, he drove in reverse then maneuvered forward through the small hole in the grass. It was hard to tell if he was on a driveway or just some abandoned road. There wasn't a mailbox or address posted anywhere. What's for certain was the horrid path wasn't meant for any vehicle with little ground clearance. It was littered with basketball-sized potholes full of mud that would have left Sam stranded if he were to haphazardly roll through one. The gravel and dirt path was barely the width of a one-lane road, consumed by tall grass that slapped the sides of Sam's car. A few sticks screeched as they slid along the doors of the sedan, but he was too focused to notice. Palmettos sprawled just beyond the waist-high grass, shaded by towering cypress and live oak trees with snaking limbs that sagged to the forest floor.

As the trail took Sam through the expanse of under-growth, he spotted a building in the distance. His car's tires splashed through puddles, though he took care to inch around the larger potholes, slowly making his way toward what he then recognized as an old wooden cabin with a dark gray tinge to it. The roof was an A-frame design, with a rusted slab of tin that peaked high in the center of the shack and slanted sharply down in the front and back. The building was raised off the ground a few feet with crumbling brick stilts to avoid water damage from flooding.

The dirt path ended in a clearing devoid of trees just in front of the shack, which extended in a circle all around the structure. Sam thought it was pretty impressive that the ancient house was still intact from first glance. The foundation appeared to bow in several directions, a sign that its structural integrity was shot.

He spotted no truck out front, but quickly had to direct his attention back to the dirt road to avoid a massive hole. A shadowy figure emerged onto the porch without Sam noticing.

After clearing the last of the holes, Sam shifted the car into park and looked up to see an elderly man wearing faded, blue jean overalls without a shirt underneath, peering at him from the porch of the house. A camouflage trucker hat sat high upon his bald head.

Sam's exhilaration died when he noticed the shotgun cradled in the man's arms, firmly tucked against his chest of curly, white hair. Vincent's house or not, Sam was readying himself to explain why he had driven down the private drive-way.

Sam opened the sedan's door and cautiously climbed out. He called out to the man, heart pounding in his chest. "Mr. Vincent Dupuis?"

The old man looked Sam up and down, staring from his leaning porch, which Sam was sure could cave in at any moment. "That depends on who's asking," the man said with a Cajun accent, further slurred by the cigarette jolting in his mouth. "So who's asking?"

Sam paused. "Uh, well, I was pointed here by a man named Lloyd at the gas station a few miles back in town." He moved closer to the porch; the man didn't seem like he was going to shoot him. He just stared blankly at Sam for a moment, presumably waiting to hear more.

Sam nervously continued. "My name is Sam Miller. My parents, Ryan and Martha Landry, died in 1988 when I was just a child. And through some court documents, I found the name of Vincent Dupuis on a form petitioning the state to gain custody of me. So I've come down here…" Sam's voice trailed off as the man quickly stepped forward. Sam stiffened, wondering if he should run, but the old man's face and demeanor changed, his wrinkles deepening as he smiled.

"Little Samuel Miller." He put his shotgun down, leaning it against the exterior wall of the house. "Boy, boy, I didn't know what kind of person was coming down here. Didn't Lloyd tell you I don't get too many visitors?"

"He certainly did."

The elderly Cajun gave out a hoarse laugh, exhaling smoke from a cigarette. "You came to the right place." Smoke lingered from his mouth as he spoke. He walked down the creaky porch steps to where Sam stood and outstretched his hand. "Vincent Dupuis," he said with a smile.

Vincent's leather-like hand gripped Sam's firmly. His handshake was strong, but welcoming, and it felt like a good omen to Sam. All along he tried to stay positive, but there was a part of him that thought he would return to Boston empty-handed. To have the mysterious Vincent Dupuis standing before him felt unreal. He cleared his throat, trying to think of what to say, but before he could respond, the old Cajun invited him inside.

"Come on, we got some things to talk about." He walked back up the stairs onto the porch, then turned back to see Sam still standing on the front lawn. "Come on now, I ain't gonna bite you."

Sam slowly followed the old man, walking up the aged stairs to the porch and through the door of the house. Almost instantly, the aroma inside the cabin hit Sam hard—a fusion of years of smoke from both cigarettes and winter fires. The same gray wood that comprised the exterior of the house made up the floor, ceiling, and walls. Some sections of the vertical slats of wood were missing from the walls, revealing insulation made from mud. Sam shuddered as he wondered what sort of critters could make their way inside the home. He assumed the front room served as the kitchen, dining area and living room, with only minimal furniture that included a yellow-green sink, refrigerator and stove, as well as a small table with two chairs. It briefly crossed his mind that the ragged house, the tiniest and simplest he had ever laid eyes on, would've been his if Vincent would've gained custody of him all those years ago. He figured he wouldn't have minded. The shack wasn't all that smaller than his apartment, anyway. And there was something charming about the old place. Home is where the heart is, people always say. And there hadn't been much heart back in his Boston home.

Vincent motioned for Sam to sit in one of the only two chairs near the square dining table. "How you like your coffee?"

Sam thought the old man's garbled Cajun accent sounded like he was quickly mumbling with a mouth full of marbles. But he managed to understand most of the sentence to give the correct response. "Black is fine." The cracked wood of the floor squeaked under Sam's feet as he sat.

Vincent rummaged around in the cluttered cabinet near the stove, clinking together dishes, and he grabbed two coffee cups. "Me and you gonna get along," Vincent said as he poured two cups of black coffee, already brewed and still hot from not long ago.

Vincent's aged home seemed to match him perfectly, Sam thought as he watched the old man. Vincent's nails were yellow, cracked, and worn. His skin was deeply bronzed and wrinkled, especially his face. His gray beard covered his neck, hanging down to his mid chest in a tangled fashion. From just a glance, Sam could tell from Vincent's hazel eyes that the Cajun had seen a lot over the years. The wrinkles around them and the leanness of his body, save for the weight positioned firmly on his stomach, told stories of years of hard work in the Louisiana heat.

Vincent sat down opposite Sam and slid over a chipped mug filled halfway with coffee across the table. The old man looked at Sam and sipped on his steaming brew, sitting calmly as if he had been expecting Sam to show up at any minute. But Sam felt uneasy, especially with the silence, so he felt he should break the ice. "Mr. Vincent, thanks for—"

But Vincent stopped Sam before he could continue.

"Don't be calling me 'Mr.' like that. You making me feel like an ole man. You can call me Vin. That's what everybody calls me. Well, what everybody I know calls me. Just don't call me a son of a bitch!"

Vincent let out a round of laughter and Sam joined in with a few low chuckles, not wanting to be rude. His mind was working overtime as he struggled to think of where to begin with questions.

"OK," Sam said as he tried to clear his mind. "Vin, thank you for the coffee."

"Well, you're welcome. Nothing accompanies a good conversation better than some coffee."

"I'm not sure where to start with all of this." Sam's right hand wrapped around the hot mug. His free hand was placed on his lap, which shook with nervousness as his stomach churned. He had so many things he wanted to say, yet he couldn't find a way to articulate them. He'd long ago come up with a plan of almost everything he wanted to ask this man when he met him, if he ever would, but in the moment, he fought to find the right words to say.

"The last time I saw you, boy, you looked quite a bit different. Couldn't even walk yet," Vincent said to spark the conversation.

"So you're really him."

Vincent nodded and smiled. "The one and only."

Sam shook his head, telling himself this moment was real despite how surreal it felt. His time in Louisiana almost up, just a random convenience store, and yet here he was with the man who could answer so many questions. His plan had actually worked. Now he wanted to know something he'd wondered for a long time.

"Are we related in anyway?"

"No, we not related. But I knew your parents very well." Vincent slurped a gulp of coffee from his ivory colored mug and leaned back in his chair. "I knew them for a long time. Since they were in their twenties. I guess not much older than you are."

"I'm twenty-five." Sam fought off a bit of disappointment that they weren't related. He shouldn't have expected any different. Evelyn had told him she and Nathan were the only relatives to be found, but he couldn't help hoping. "That's right. Born in, what, January of 1988, if I remember right."

"Yeah, that's right." Sam was surprised that Vincent remembered such a small detail about his life. He figured Nathan didn't even know the year he was born, let alone the month. But all these years later, and Vincent did. That either meant the old man simply had a sharp memory, or that he was once a part—perhaps a big part—of Sam's life.

Vincent leaned over the table closer to Sam and squinted before sitting back in his chair. "You got your mother's eyes."

"Really?" he said, his voice quivering. His eyes glossed over with tears.

"Aw, yeah. She had beautiful blue eyes just like you. On a sunny day, you could see them things from a mile away. Ryan always said he would get lost in them. Would you like to see a picture of the two of them?"

Sam nodded slightly, unable to speak. He had never seen a photograph of his parents before, and his emotions were hitting him strongly. He assumed that if he talked at length about them he wouldn't be able to stop himself from crying.

Vincent stood and disappeared into the back room, which, from Sam's vantage point, looked as bare bones as virtually everything inside the shack did. Vincent returned and offered him the faded photograph.

Sam delicately took it into his own hands.

"There on the right is me, your momma is in the middle and that's your daddy on the left," Vincent said as he pointed at the photograph. "And of course, the little guy your momma is holding is you. I remember the day we took that picture. They had just had one of their best days fishing all season. Your daddy hauled in more crawfish that day than I've seen anybody catch in a long time."

A tear streamed down Sam's cheek as he looked at his father, then his mother and then to Vincent, before looking back to his father. For years he dreamed of what his parents looked like. Turns out, they weren't much different than he imagined. His mother was a short woman with a dainty figure, accompanied by a head full of light blonde hair that draped past her shoulders. She had a button nose and a warm smile. She had Sam wrapped in a blue blanket, his face just barely visible. Sam's father sported a short beard surrounding defined cheekbones and was also thin, but about a foot taller than Martha. Ryan's long blonde hair hung down to his shoulders—it reminded Sam of his own. Both Ryan's and Martha's outfits were soiled, matching their dark, summer tans. Vincent seemed to have a few more teeth in the photograph. Other than that, his appearance looked mostly unchanged. He was still sporting a gray beard and dressed, more or less, in the same attire.

Vincent peered at the photograph from over Sam's shoulder. "Ryan was a hell of a fisherman. And Martha had one of the best gardens around. A green thumb? More like a green hand she had." The old man sat back in his chair.

"They look so happy." Sam's voice was scratchy from holding back more tears. He never would've guessed he would be crying in front of Vincent. But years of emotions were bubbling to the surface, further fueled by the sight of his parents in the faded photograph he held in his hands.

"They were happy. You were born just a few months before that picture was taken, I believe. They had everything they ever wanted in life at that time."

"I've wondered what they were like for so long. It's almost like I made up my own personalities for them, you know? I created in my head what I thought they were like. What would've made them laugh? What would they have taught me?"

"They were some of the best people I ever knew. I can tell you that. Your father was one of the most dependable young men I've had the pleasure of knowing."

Tears rolled uncontrollably down Sam's face. He couldn't hold them back any longer. He tried to speak, but felt a sob building in his throat. He clamped down on it and took in slow breaths to control himself. After a lengthy exhale, he spoke. "How did you know them?"

"I met them in the early '80s when they first moved to the bayou. At that time, I was living in the Basin just a few miles from them. They bought their house from an ole man's wife after he passed away. Boy oh boy, they didn't know much about commercial fishing. Sure, they knew how to hunt, fish, and garden. But living in the Basin and making a living out of it ain't no walk in the park."

Sam wiped the tears from his eyes while coughing to

clear his throat. He looked at Vincent for the first time since the old man had handed the photograph to him. "What's the Basin?"

"The Atchafalaya (At-cha-fuh-lie-uh) Basin. Largest swamp in the country. Them levees you drove by right before you turned to come back here hold back all the water from it. Your parents lived in that swamp for years. A lot of people did that, you see, even though it was tough after the levees were built."

"Why?" Sam asked.

"Well, the levees hold floodwater in the Basin during the spring, while keeping everything else outside the levees dry, and then the water is flushed into the Gulf of Mexico through the river. In the early 1930's, when those levees were built, the floods got worse until the high water forced a lot of the ole Cajuns out the Basin. A few families stayed over the years, but a lot left, and hardly anyone, except some ole fishermen, live there now. I was born out there. I stayed until right after your parents died, but I finally left the swamp."

"Left the swamp? Then what do you call where you live now? All the areas I drove by on the way in here looked half-way underwater."

Vincent laughed. "Yeah, a lot of the land around here is low swampland. But all of this water is runoff from rain and there's usually a road to take you to any high ground. In the Atchafalaya, the swamp water comes from the Atchafalaya River and it can rise in an instant. It's more unpredictable and wilder out there. And there ain't no roads. It's basically like a big, long and skinny wilderness surrounded by a ring of levees."

"No kidding. So my parents were Cajun fishermen.

When I found out they were from Louisiana, I always just guessed they were Cajun. I never knew for sure. I didn't suspect they fished for a living, though."

"They were about as Cajun as they come. Well, with a last name like Landry, that's Louisiana Cajun royalty, boy."

Sam laughed a bit and Vincent smirked back.

"You know, I didn't think I'd even find you out here," Sam said. "I'm still shocked we're sitting here talking and I'm looking at a picture of my parents. I guess I half expected to go home having found nothing."

"The world has its way of working things out, I've come to learn that over the years," Vincent said with a smile.

From the way the old man sat, looking delicately at Sam from across the small table, it appeared as if he was waiting to answer more questions. Sam took the cue and, having gained some composure, continued. "I guess the main thing I've always wondered is what happened to them?"

Vincent shifted in his seat and looked at the gray, wooden floor. "I'll never forget the day. They both went out one afternoon for a boat ride and never came back." He looked up, meeting Sam's eyes. "A big tropical storm came through—tore down trees, uprooted them, and messed up a bunch of people's houses. Your daddy knew the bayous, lakes, and canals better than I did, I think. Man, he was a fast learner. But he must have lost his way in all that rain and wind, trying to make it back home. What I think happened is he hit a log underwater and they both flew out the boat. But I don't know for sure. All I could ever find was the boat."

Both men, now holding back tears, sat in silence for a

few moments, until Vincent mustered the courage to continue. "If they would've had life jackets on, they maybe would've lived. I found both their life jackets in the boat, so I assumed they weren't wearing them. They were in a big body of deep, deep water near the river. With the waves and confusion, it must've been too much for them."

Sam couldn't respond at first. He stared off into the distance, staving off tears. After several deep, slow breaths, he thought he could speak without breaking down. "So that's it," he said through a few lingering tears, "that's how they died."

"One of the saddest days of my life. It still gets to me when I think about it. And seeing you, with your momma's eyes and a spitting image of your daddy, boy, it's like I'm looking at both of them right here in front of me."

Sam dried his face with his shirt sleeve and cleared his throat. "So I wasn't with them, then? I wasn't with them on the boat?"

"You were with me."

Sam looked up at Vincent with another question, the one he had wondered about since he found the old man's name. Before Sam could think of the words to ask, Vincent answered his unspoken question. "I tried to keep you. Your parents were so young that they never made a will to list a guardian. But they always said if something ever happened to them, they wanted me to raise you. Damn court didn't think I was fit to raise a child because of this ole house and my age. But I guess they did the best thing they knew how and gave you to your relatives."

Sam replayed Vincent's words in his head: 'the best thing they knew how.' If they had only known, he thought.

"I never figured I would ever see you again," Vincent continued. "I wish you could've been here all these years, where you belonged."

Sam didn't think he belonged anywhere. Yet, here was this stranger, who seemed to care about him deeply, telling him so. "How old was I when they died?"

"Just a little baby. Only about six months old. Next to having to say goodbye to your parents, not knowing what was going to happen to you was the hardest thing. It ate me up for years."

Sam sat in silence. Anymore questions seemed to escape him as he analyzed everything he was told. The photograph, imagining how his parents died, Vincent telling him he belonged in Louisiana—he tried to make sense of all of it.

"What happened to you, anyway?" Vincent said after the period of silence. "Where'd you end up?"

"My mother's only relatives were given custody of me. So after a few weeks I spent in an orphanage, they came down from Boston and moved me up there. I've pretty much never left there since."

"Boston? Boy, that's a long way away from this place. Well, what about the people that took you in, they told you about Ryan and Martha?"

"I was never told anything about them, really. Hell, I don't think they knew anything about them, anyway. All I learned was their names and they were from down here."

"That's a shame they couldn't tell you anything."

"Yeah. Evelyn was related to Martha, but she had only seen her a time or two. She died when I was nine, but before she did she told me about them. I didn't even know Ryan and Martha were my real parents up to that point."

Vincent raised his eyebrows. "I'm sorry to hear that, about Evelyn."

"It's OK. It was a long time ago."

"Was, what's his name...her husband, what's he think about you coming down here?"

"Nathan. He and I haven't spoken since I was seventeen. To be honest, I'm not sure if he's even alive anymore." Sam winced a little as he said the words, knowing the pitying look he'd probably get from Vincent.

Vincent's facial expression showed he was taken aback. Sam could tell the old man wanted to know more, but he wanted to change the subject. He wasn't there to talk about what he'd been through during his life. So he switched gears to focus back on his parents. "I'm sorry for getting emotional. I didn't expect that to happen. This all just kind of took me by surprise, I guess."

Vincent took the final swig from his coffee mug.

In an attempt to be a polite guest, Sam took his first sip of coffee, which was cold from sitting for so long. But he hadn't really been thinking about coffee during their conversation.

"Hey, no need to say you sorry," Vincent said. He stood and put his empty mug into the sink. "That must be cold, you want me to pour you a fresh cup?"

"No, thanks, this is fine."

Vincent nodded and sat back down at the table. "Well, I'm glad you here."

"Me too." Sam leaned back in his chair and rubbed his face, pushing his fingers through his blond hair. "This is a lot to take in already, though, and I've got so little time," he said, exhaling loudly.

"How much time you got?"

"I leave tomorrow afternoon."

Vincent stood, walked toward the entrance of his house, and opened the door. "We got some time. Instead of just sitting here and telling you about them, I'm gonna show you who they were."

Three

S am sat shotgun in Vincent's old jalopy, its body riddled with dents and accentuated with rings of rust. In places where rust hadn't taken over, the old truck sported a royal blue hue, one that Sam figured was surely more handsome years before. The color had turned matte, lacking the shine of a fresh paint job. Vincent said the aged Ford pickup, which he had dubbed 'Ole Blue,' was older than Sam.

The pair moved at a crawl down the bayou road, a pace that was fine for Sam. He figured the truck engine, which clacked loudly the faster Vincent drove, might give out if pushed to a faster speed, anyway. The snail's pace allowed him to really get a good view of the swampland he had sped past on the way in.

Sam peered outside the window, amazed how the landscape was so incredibly lush, an impenetrable barrier of green vegetation that stood just beyond the edge of the asphalt. The oppressive heat engulfed his entire body, penetrating down into his bones. Even so, he didn't mind it. He thought it was a welcome variation from Boston's weather.

Vincent had his prized possession in tow: a homemade Cajun skiff. The unpainted aluminum boat glistened in the

Southern sunlight as it jolted and bounced on a trailer far too big for it. Its bow came to an abrupt point, a feature Vincent said helped the vessel navigate through aquatic vegetation and trees, as well as break through waves. It was eighteen feet long but only three feet wide, with a solid black outboard motor fastened to the stern.

"I made that thing way back in 1973," Vincent said of his boat as he drove. "For years we used wooden boats. But that was my first metal one. Back then, if you wanted something nice like that, you had to make it yourself. There wasn't all these factory-made boats that you could just buy on a whim."

Vincent beamed as he talked of his skiff. Sam had never seen anyone so proud of something. "I've rode in it through hurricanes and floods, from all the way to the south end of the Basin to the north. I fished for crawfish, catfish, gators—just about anything you can catch and sell, I did it."

While Sam listened to Vincent continue on about the boat, he kept eying the levee to his left. He could barely make out the green tips of trees behind the earthen wall. He wondered what it looked like just on the other side, this place where his parents had apparently lived. The man-made hills stood about forty feet high in most places, gently sloping upward into the sky. In some spots, fences housed cattle that grazed on the acres of lush grass that covered them. The bumps in the landscape were the only elevation change found anywhere for hundreds of miles. Vincent recalled that for some Louisianans, the only hills they ever saw were the levees of the Atchafalaya or the ones a few miles east that lined the Mississippi River.

"So, I'm a bit curious, Vin," Sam said, his arm hanging

out of the window, his fingers drumming on the outside of Ole Blue. "Where exactly are we going?"

Vincent smiled. "You'll see in just a second. I promise."

"Today has been full of surprises. What's one more to add to the list?"

"Well, you won't have to wait too much longer." Vincent guided his truck off the road paralleling the levee. He made a sharp left turn up a crude, gravel path shooting up to the top of the man-made hill.

They jostled up the levee, and Sam sat up as high as he could on the truck's bench seat, waiting for his first glimpse of what these engineering marvels held back. Vincent's truck whined as it climbed, with a pop and a crackle bellowing out the machine's tailpipe as the gas pedal was pressed farther toward the floorboard. As the pair peaked on top of the levee, Sam's eyes widened. "Wow," he breathed as he looked out over miles and miles of green, what he thought seemed like an endless supply of forest. The tops of the trees subtly swayed in the wind, and puffy, white clouds floated overhead yet caused no concern for rain.

"Welcome to the Atchafalaya Basin. Now, I'm gonna really show you Louisiana," Vincent said with a proud, near toothless grin as he drove his truck down the path. He pulled through the gravel parking lot, putting his boat into position to launch it into a canal parallel to the base of the levee. He backed the boat down the slanted concrete launch into the water virtually without looking. The old Cajun stopped and got out of Ole Blue with Sam following close behind.

"What river or lake...or whatever is this?" Sam asked as he trailed Vincent to the rear of the truck.

"It's the Intracoastal Canal. It follows the levee from the

Gulf of Mexico to Baton Rouge. Barges use it to ship goods from the Mississippi River down south. We going over there." Vincent pointed out into the distance.

Sam gazed toward the open water and trees with a blank stare. Without a road or building anywhere around, it was a sight his city-slicker eyes had never seen before.

Vincent looked at Sam's awed facial expression and laughed. "You'll see. It ain't as scary as it looks," he said to reassure him. Vincent picked up a rope that was attached to the front of his boat and handed it to Sam. "Hold this here. Don't let it go now, or you gonna have to go swimming. I'm gonna back up a little bit more so the boat floats, then I'm gonna pull back up. You just hold the boat right here by the bank until I get back."

Sam waited near the water's edge, rope in hand, and did as Vincent instructed. Once Vincent parked Ole Blue near a handful of other trucks with empty boat trailers, he returned to Sam. "You ready?"

"As ready as I can be."

Vincent climbed into his boat, walked to the stern, and cranked the motor. A plume of white smoke burst out of the engine as it rattled to life. He took a small box of matches out of his chest pocket on the overalls he was wearing and lit a cigarette he had been holding on top his ear. He then plopped down on a milk crate and took long puffs on his cigarette. Sam watched as Vincent didn't blow out to exhale, but rather let the smoke slowly seep out of his mouth and nostrils. When the old man talked, smoke made its way to the air. "Come on, now. Come in and sit on that green crate right here." He pointed to another milk crate.

Sam climbed aboard and awkwardly walked a few steps

with careful balance. He waddled a few more paces as the boat swayed from side to side. He barely managed to sit on the plastic crate without falling over.

Vincent smiled after watching him. "You'll get your sea legs sooner or later." He reversed away from the boat landing and pointed the bow of the boat toward a large opening on the other side of the 100-yard-wide canal. He throttled and steered, not with a steering wheel, but by a long tiller handle shaped like a pole that stuck out from the side of the motor. They started picking up speed across the body of water.

Sam sat facing the front of the boat, his hair fluttering wildly in the wind as his head whipped in several directions scanning his surroundings. The breeze ripped tears from his eyes, making him blink. The Intracoastal was wide, long and straight, bordered by trees on all sides. When Vincent steered into the smaller body of water across the canal, he yelled above the cry of his sputtering motor, "This is Little Bayou Pigeon. It dumps water from the interior swamp into the canal we just left. It'll take you wherever you want to go around here."

Little Bayou Pigeon didn't resemble the Intracoastal Canal, which was man-made and dug deep and straight for industrial use. This body of water naturally bowed and turned in varying directions. The old Cajun kept a moderate pace as he navigated the winding bayou, but he didn't speak. Neither did Sam. It didn't seem like a time for words. The beauty and wildness, in a way, spoke enough for the both of them.

Bald cypress trees, even larger than Sam had seen on his way into Bayou Pigeon, graced the muddy waters of the bayou's bank. Abundant vegetation like cattail sprawled near the cypress, and lily pads the size of dinner plates floated along the surface of the water, occasionally making their way toward the center of the bayou. Birds flew in almost every direction, lazily hovering just above the towering cypress, landing in the water, or in a tree—it didn't seem to matter to them where they flew. There were hordes of them, white egrets of all sizes, flying in packs across the sky. Larger great blue herons, though fewer, gracefully stood near the bayou's banks in the grass, pecking at the water for a snack. Sam was waiting to see houses or piers, some sign of humanity along the bayou. But after each curve, there were only more trees sagging over the bayou.

For a majority of the outing, Sam and Vincent had this section of swamp to themselves. The solitude made Sam wonder how only a levee separated all of what he was seeing from civilization. On one side, houses lined the levee and a few hundred people lived within a ten-minute boat drive from where they were. On the other side, there was a vast wilderness. He noticed that the air even smelled different within the Atchafalaya, like a strong aroma of pollen from flowers and trees, interspersed with a fishy smell that crept through every so often. It was such a stark difference, he thought, from anything else he'd ever experienced.

Vincent's skiff glided over the smooth, brown-stained water with ease. He skillfully dodged logs and occasional mats of floating lilies or bouquets of water hyacinth that blocked a section of the bayou. A boat finally passed them in a skiff not much different from Vincent's. Vincent steered into the crisp waves created from the passing boater and his skiff cut through them just like he said it would.

Vincent crisscrossed bayous, man-made canals, and even a small lake or two, navigating without a map and as casually as one would drive a car through a neighborhood. He had been down this way many a time or two, Sam suspected. The old man's beard flew back in the wind, yet he still somehow managed to keep his cigarette lit.

Though Sam had never been in such wilderness, much less a boat before, he felt at ease with Vincent. The nervousness that had enveloped him for the majority of the trip started to dissipate. It was strange, but he knew he was in safe hands. Whether it was Vincent's welcoming personality, the fact that the he knew Ryan and Martha so well or both, Sam didn't know yet.

After the pair cruised for a half hour, winding through the different parts of the Atchafalaya, Vincent turned down a long, straight canal cutting through a field of cypress. Not far down the canal, Vincent slowed and drove the skiff over to a small opening in the right bank. It wasn't much of a path, but rather a small stream between the trees. Vincent throttled his boat slowly forward. All Sam could see ahead was water, trees, then more of the same. He looked back at Vincent and the old man sat still on his milk crate, as calm as ever.

It appeared as if the pair had hit a dead end, but Vincent apparently didn't think so. The water was so shallow Vincent had to trim up his motor, raising it until the propeller was barely submerged. They churned up mud and sticks as the propeller made contact with the soft bottom of the swamp. Vincent revved the outboard motor and twisted it from side to side via the tiller handle. The boat zigzagged in place and more mud spewed out from under the water, but slowly they inched forward deeper into the stand of cypress, leaving behind the open water of the canal, until they were immersed under the shade of the tree canopy. The trunks, almost perfectly straight as they rose into the sky, were only inches from the sides of the boat, so close Sam could touch them.

Without the whine of the boat motor, Sam noticed the Atchafalaya came to life. Noises of all sorts filled the muggy air. Frogs, cicadas, and birds chirped, buzzed, and pecked seemingly in unison like a fine-tuned orchestra. It wasn't the quiet Sam was expecting.

Eventually, the distance between the side of the boat and the trees grew, until a sizable stream took shape, getting wider the farther Sam and Vincent traveled. The small stream grew into a bayou about forty yards wide, deep enough for Vincent to trim his motor back down and drive with ease. Trees still towered over the boat, Spanish moss hanging on their branches, stretching out in front of the boat like a curtain, and casting a dark shadow over the water.

White birds sat perched in trees or rested in the shallow water near the shore. Sheets of green slime matted parts of the water's surface, swirling as the boat passed over it. The water wasn't a deep brown like it had been in the other bodies of water Vincent had driven through. Here, rather, it was a shade of black, the result of low levels of oxygen in the water. The bayou twisted and turned, so much so that Sam couldn't see more than a hundred yards in front of him before it jetted in another direction.

As they traveled farther, the vegetation lining the bayou changed. Instead of only cypress, large live oaks with finger-like branches sat perched on high ground to the left and right of the boat. The old branches extended so far that some sagged to the forest floor, while others extended out over the water. They, too, were adorned with Spanish moss that dangled on nearly every branch and twig.

The men rounded a turn and as Sam looked toward Vincent, he saw the old man smiling. Vincent nodded without speaking, motioning for Sam to look toward the bow. When he turned his head, at first, he didn't quite know what he was looking at. He knew it was a man-made building, near the right side of the bank about fifty yards ahead—the first he had spotted since he got in the boat. However, the structure appeared to be floating, with one half sagging in the black water badly. It was a houseboat, but one that had seen better days.

"Where are we?" Sam said, the first words shared in a half-hour.

"We in Riley Bayou, long forgotten by anybody who once used it." Vincent pointed to the aged houseboat before continuing. "And that there is the real reason we out here. It's the houseboat where you were born."

Sam looked at Vincent, then back at the aged building. "Where I was born?"

"That's where your momma and daddy lived. Ole Vin lived about a few yards further down. Hell, about six of us lived down here at one point before the oil company dug that canal back there and cut off the bayou."

"This was actually my parent's house?" Sam said, astonished at the sight of the building. He noticed the yellow exterior was faded badly and missing chunks of paint here and there. The roof, much like on Vincent's old shack, was comprised of rusted sections of tin.

"Worth the surprise, huh?" Vincent said.

"When you said they lived in the swamp I never pictured it like this. This is in the middle of nowhere. You can't even get here by a vehicle."

Vincent laughed. "I told you, the Basin is a wild place."

"How'd you all live out here?"

"A lot of patience and hard work."

Vincent motored toward the structure and positioned his boat parallel to the home. The front porch was bounded with a thin, mesh screen made of metal, with a wooden walkway that extended about two feet and encircled the entire home. The back end of the entire houseboat sunk into the water about a foot. It sat not far from the bank of the bayou, secured in place with ropes tied to nearby trees. It was a small structure, just thirty feet long and ten feet wide, looking more like a shed than a home.

"Grab the post right there and tie us off," Vincent said.

Sam eased his way to the front of the boat.

"Be careful, now. I haven't walked on this ole thing in a few months. Go on now, step up," Vincent continued.

Sam got out and onto the badly weathered floorboards on the walkway, where the wood was partly or completely missing. He stood and held the boat steady so Vincent could climb aboard as well. Scattered along the ceiling were wasp nests full of an alarming number of the creatures. One buzzed next to Sam's head and sent him ducking.

"You dancing or something?" Vincent said with a playful grin as he climbed out of the boat. "I haven't had the energy to keep up with it after the Basin was flooded a few years ago, much less clean these wasps outta here. And the last hurricane really did a number on this ole thing."

"It's definitely seen its better days."

"It got harder and harder to keep it looking nice all these years."

The door that once covered the entrance to the screened-in porch was missing. Vincent walked in with Sam close behind, both the men dodging floorboards that looked like they might give way if stepped on. A torn screen door a few feet ahead was all that separated the inside of the home from the harsh Louisiana elements. Vincent pushed open the front door, making the hinges squeak, and they walked in. The initial view of the interior reminded Sam of Vincent's old house back across the levee, with a simple design containing only two rooms, though it was much dirtier. Ahead on the floor were scattered paper, books and a few boxes, all with a layer of filth on them that didn't seem like simple scrubbing would remove. The sunlight jetted through a cracked window missing several pieces of glass and sliced through the room at an angle, reverberating off the dusty floor and off-white walls.

As Sam stepped farther into the room, he heard a crunch under his foot. He reached down and picked up what was left of a photograph frame. "These are my parents, right?" He pointed to two people in a badly faded, black and white snapshot.

Vincent peered over at the photograph. "That's them, alright. Who you think took that picture?"

"You did?"

"Well, of course," Vincent said as he walked to the sink that sat atop a pair of cabinets, rubbing his hand on the dirt-caked porcelain. "Your momma and daddy couldn't get me out this house when you were born." He gave Sam an almost embarrassed smile. Looking over the place, he shook his head. "And it's been even harder for me to keep thieves out a place like this. Even though not many people know this thing is here, over the years they trickled in and took something here or there. I tried to bring some stuff back with me to my ole house, but I hated doing that. For some reason I just wanted everything in here like it was when they left."

Sam was starting to see how deeply Vincent truly cared for his parents. The old man spoke of them with reverence even after all these years. And even though Sam had been with Vincent for only a few hours, he knew that compassion extended to him, a complete stranger. Of course, he figured that was probably because Vincent didn't see him as a stranger.

Sam wiped the grime off of the photograph of his parents, and set it upright on the counter. "So, Vin, you guys all lived down here away from everything, right. So how'd you make money?"

"Well, we'd fish throughout the day and drive to a little shack on the other side of the Basin, just outside the levees, to sell our catch. Some days, we'd sell to boaters passing up and down the main bayous. But the best thing was bartering, not selling for money. We got money for things like gas, but if we could barter, that was the best. Your momma would jar wild blackberries, and I'm telling you, it was the best jam I've ever eaten. She could have bartered for anything in Louisiana with that."

"Isn't that something," Sam said, shaking his head. "I really couldn't have imagined a more different life that they lived. And to think that I would've grown up in this place." Sam focused his attention to the back room. "Is that the bedroom back there?"

"Yeah, go on, walk back if you'd like. Just be careful. I don't know if any of these boards might give way on that side. It's sagging pretty bad."

Sam walked to the other end of the small home toward a half closed, brown door. He pushed it open and walked in the slanted room. Though it was a bedroom, it housed no bed or any other furniture—it was barren except for a few papers strewn on the floor. Light from a small window in the middle of the back wall was barely enough for Sam to see where to step. He tiptoed around the room to ensure the floorboards were steady enough to stand on. They were covered with the same filth as the front part of the home. There was a bathroom in the right corner of the room that had no door, just a curtain to separate it. Sam peeked his head in the dark room where he could barely make out a cracked bathtub.

Before Sam exited the room he spotted a photograph of an elderly couple on the wall to the left of the doorway, which he thought might've been his grandparents. He looked on the other side behind the door to see if another photograph was hidden. He found a painting of a night in the swamp, displaying a full moon reflected off the surface of water surrounded by the cypress that were so abundant in the Atchafalaya. The painting had bright purples and deep reds to mimic the moment the sun sets and night starts to take over. Sam noticed a signature in the corner of the painting and he leaned in closer to get a better look in the dark room. It was the signature of Martha Landry.

Sam grabbed the painting off the wall and walked back into the first room. "She painted this? This is absolutely beautiful."

Vincent squinted to see what Sam held. "Yeah, she sure did. If she wasn't out helping your daddy with the traps or in the garden, she'd sit out on that front porch and paint."

"Are there any others like this just lying around? I mean, what's all left here?"

"I'm not completely sure. There might be a few things in those boxes. Thieves took all the tools and things they could sell. There wasn't much in here to begin with, though. They both made do with as little as possible."

"That's a shame. A shame people stole their stuff, I mean. But, I guess I can't say I'm not surprised. I've seen people do worse."

"I figure the last big flood we had in 2011 took some stuff with it, too. I came back here and secured it the best I could. Water got a few inches in the house, and when it receded it made the back end of this thing sag like it's doing now. The Basin never used to flood so bad until they put them levees out here and that flood gate on the river. When they open the flood gates in high water years, it saves Baton Rouge and New Orleans from flooding, but it sure creates some kind of headache for us out here."

Sam sat the painting down on the kitchen table and leaned against the counter. "The more questions I ask you, the more questions I have," he said with a slight laugh.

"I guess that's how it goes sometimes, huh?"

"I bet it was tough for them to live out here—it had to be."

"In many ways it was. But you got used to it, you know? It became a part of your life after so long to where you just didn't notice how tough it really was. Plus, I know having you in their lives made it so much better."

"Is that picture of that elderly couple in the bedroom one of their parents?"

Vincent walked to the back room, and poked his head around the door. "Yep." He walked back to lean against the cabinet. "That was Ryan's momma and daddy. He was real close to his momma. His daddy died when he was just a little kid. So he was practically raised just by her."

Sam hesitated before asking, knowing it was a long shot. "Did they ever have any visitors or anyone come by that you might have suspected was family?"

"Not that I know of. I'm not sure anyone knew they lived in the Basin other than the few of us down Riley Bayou. I know Ryan's parents were both gone whenever he moved to the Basin. And I'm pretty sure Martha's were, too. I can't be too sure because she didn't really talk about it much. We had a funeral for them back in Breaux Bridge, where your momma was from. Aside from the few friends and everyone that lived down Riley Bayou, I don't think there was any relatives there."

A pang of sorrow hit Sam's heart as he thought about his parents' funeral. Learning so much about them, meeting Vincent, and adventuring out into the Basin had turned this day into an exciting one, and it made it easier to forget that, no matter what, Ryan and Martha were gone. He wished, like he often did, that things were different.

"That must have been a rough day. You never found their bodies, though, right? So, what did you all do for the funeral?"

"I tried for as long as I could, but no. We purchased a little plot for both of them in Breaux Bridge, anyway. The headstone has both of their names carved on it. Me and the others from the bayou buried little trinkets we thought were important. I put in a necklace your parents gave me on a birthday."

"How far is that from here?"

"I guess a little more than an hour and a half from here to the west."

"I'd like to visit their plot one day."

"You say the word and I'll gladly take you."

"Where's Henderson, the town my father was from?"

"Not far from Breaux Bridge. Henderson is nestled up to the levee on the other end of the Basin. At first, I never knew for sure why they decided to leave home and move to the Basin like they did. I always thought they might've been trying to escape something back home. Turned out I was right."

Sam stood up straight. "What do you mean? What were they trying to escape?"

"For your daddy, he just didn't have any family. After his momma died, he figured he had nothing left. He was looking for an excuse to escape reality when your momma came along. And for her, well, she didn't have much family to begin with, I don't think. She never really talked about her family much, but she was looking for an adventure and found that in your daddy."

Vincent looked up, smiled, and shook his head. "Then when they met me, I think I helped make up their mind."

"Did you convince them to move out here or something?"

Vincent smirked. "I might've persuaded them." The old man leaned back, which Sam recognized as the signal he was preparing to delve into a story. "I'll never forget the day I met them. They both came through Riley Bayou real early one morning. They were looking for a good spot to go set some traps. When they saw my houseboat, they came right up to the front porch where I was drinking coffee. I invited them in and we visited a little while. They were living at a camp on the edge of the swamp near Henderson and had been looking for a way to move into the Basin. I told them this ole thing was for sale and they moved in the next day."

Sam imagined his father and mother moving into the houseboat, just the two of them living in the swamp together. "Did they find the adventure they were looking for?"

"I know your momma did. She got a kick out of living out here. For Ryan, I think this place soothed his soul. It's what it does, you know. He'd go sit out on the edge of a lake and watch the sunrise, sometimes by himself, and just think." Vincent stuck a cigarette in his mouth and lit it with a match. He slowly exhaled as he spoke. "He would talk to me about it sometimes. He said he couldn't explain the way he felt out here, but something about the wilderness, the trees—everything—made him feel complete. He said moving out here was the easiest decision he ever made in his life. Ole Vin can definitely agree with that."

"Well then how'd you end up in Bayou Pigeon? Why didn't you stay out here?"

Vincent looked up at Sam, deep sadness in his soft eyes. "It made ole Vin too sad to be out here without them. Plus, I figured it would help me get custody of you if the court knew I wasn't living in the Basin. Didn't help none." He shrugged.

Sam felt unexpected tears rushing to his eyes. He walked away from Vincent and picked up the photograph. The tears made it hard to see the faded image, especially with the waning light. The sun was dipping beneath the trees and the last rays of sunlight were disappearing from the bayou.

Vincent peered out one of the windows. "I know we just got here, but we gonna have to head back. We can come back in the morning, if you'd like. You can finish looking around and search through those boxes."

"Yeah, that'd be nice, Vin."

"You need a place to stay for the night?"

"Well, I've been staying at a hotel back in Plaquemine."

"Nonsense, you gonna stay with me tonight. Ain't no use in driving all the way over there tonight then back here tomorrow."

"You sure?"

"Well of course. We gonna go a little ways down the bayou and stay at my buddy's camp. Then we can come back first thing tomorrow morning so you can look around some more."

Sam nodded his head in approval. "That sounds like a plan."

"Alright, then let's go before we sink into the water in this ole thing," Vincent said as he made his way out the front door.

While Sam wanted to slip the old photograph that he held in his pocket, he could see what Vincent meant about not wanting to remove anything from the house. He thought the memory belonged there. So he placed the faded photograph back onto the kitchen counter, positioning it so his parents faced the entry to the houseboat. He exited the screen door and joined Vincent back in the skiff, just as the last rays of sunshine reflected off the surface of Riley Bayou.

Four

Vincent and Sam arrived at a small island after driving the skiff through Grand Lake, a slender body of water about fifteen miles as the crow flies southwest of Riley Bayou. The oblong slice of land, one of many dotting the lake, was a dense patch of woods. The only hint of man's presence anywhere in sight was a flutter of yellow light jetting out of a window from a hunting and fishing camp, used as a temporary stay rather than a permanent residence for Vincent's friend Chris.

"Do you always drive in the dark like that?" Sam asked as he prepared to tie the rope attached to the bow of the skiff to a pier. The rope was thick and rough, making it tough to manipulate. He struggled with it for a bit, but finally got it tied under Vincent's watchful eye.

"Just when it's a full moon like it is right now. Don't need a light when you can see real good like this."

Sam nodded. Though the moon made it easier to see the swamp without the aid of lights, it didn't ease his nerves throughout the dark drive.

Sam looked up at Chris' small camp from inside the boat. It was a tiny, square structure that sat up high on the shore of the island on thick, wooden stilts. The shack was barely fifteen feet wide and sat ten feet in the air to avoid being flooded in high water years. The plywood exterior wasn't painted, and gave it the appearance that it had been fastened together on a short weekend.

"Chris is a good ole boy," Vincent said as he turned off his boat motor. "You'll like him. He's a real nice fella—always willing to lend a helping hand. I been knowing him since he was not much older than you." The old man took the lead up the stairs to Chris' raised camp.

As the pair got closer, the sound of a running motor grew to an almost deafening level. Sam guessed it was coming from the porch of the camp. It drowned out the buzzes and hums of the wildlife lurking around the shack. "What's that noise?" he asked.

"Ah, that's Chris' generator he's got running. Ain't got no power lines out here. If you want electricity, you got to have a generator."

Vincent knocked on Chris' door and quickly entered without waiting for a response. "What the hell you doing, boy?" he announced as he walked in like he owned the place.

Sam entered to find man, who he assumed was Chris, only wearing underwear and sprawled on a tan sofa, the upholstery missing in spots and revealing yellow chunks of cushion, with an empty bottle of liquor sitting atop his chest.

"Vin?" Chris uttered with one eye open as he struggled to lift his head up.

"Yeah, it's me. Damn, boy, you a mess, huh?"

"Nah, I just was relaxing, man," Chris, who sported a high and tight haircut and a neatly trimmed goatee, said in a confused fashion as he attempted to sit up. He was solidly built, a little over 6-foot-tall with plenty of body mass.

"Don't get up. We gonna be fine," Vincent said as he motioned for Sam to close the door. "We came to spend the night. We'll be quiet, just go back to sleep."

"No, no, I'm gonna get up," Chris insisted. He sat up, and leaned his head against the side of the sofa. His entire right arm was covered in tattoos, with a large one gracing the left side of his chest that read *Semper Fidelis* in cursive letters. He squinted his eyes, and pointed at Sam. "Who's that?"

"That's Sam. He's a family friend I got visiting."

Sam felt awfully uncomfortable watching Chris. The man sat in a state of delirium and the aroma of alcohol was so strong that he felt the urge to step outside for some fresh air. Just the smell was enough to bring back memories of nights he'd rather forget.

Vincent walked over to Chris and threw a blanket over him while Sam walked back outside onto the porch. A few moments later, Vincent opened the door and stuck his head outside to see Sam leaning against a post, staring off into the night.

"Got Chris settled down again. You alright, boy? What you came out here for?"

Sam turned to Vincent. "I'm fine, just felt like I was intruding, I guess."

"Ah, no, that's just Chris for you." Vincent shook his head, laughed, and motioned Sam to return. "Sorry, he ain't always drunk like that. Come back inside. Now, let's see what we got here."

Sam walked back inside as Vincent opened the fridge and found it devoid of anything edible. The old man turned to examine the contents of an ice chest nearby. He dug around the cold, slushy ice and pulled out a loaf of bread and a saturated pack of ham.

"I guess we not eating too good tonight," he said as he held up the dripping food to Sam. "But we eating and that's good enough."

Vincent placed four pieces of bread on paper towels on Chris' fold-up card table. Besides the couch Chris slept on and another nearby, the only other furniture in the room included the table and mini-fridge, as well a set of cabinets with a sink.

"Oh that's OK, Vin," Sam said in a whisper. "Whatever is fine with me. I'm not a picky eater. Do you need some help making those?"

"I got it. And don't worry about making noise. He ain't gonna wake up." Vincent slammed his foot on the floor with a loud thud. He peaked his head over the couch. "See, he ain't even moved."

Sam sat on a stool near Vincent. "Do you stay here a lot?"

"Just when I'm too lazy to go back across the levee. Hell, I helped him build this place. He better not mind me coming stay." Vincent pulled a jar of mayonnaise from the ice chest and lathered the bread with it.

"So he was a Marine?"

"How'd you guess that?"

"I saw the semper fi tattoo on his chest. It's a Marine phrase. Plus, his haircut is a dead giveaway."

"Oh, yeah, that's right. Well, yeah, he sure was. He went over to Iraq twice. That's a brave S.O.B right there." He paused from making the sandwiches, grabbed two orange-flavored sodas from the ice chest, and handed one to Sam.

"So, what kinda plan you got coming way down here and looking for me, anyway?"

Sam cracked open the can and took a sip. "What do you mean?"

"Well, I imagine that you had some type of plan coming to Louisiana."

"It wasn't much of a plan. I just asked a bunch of people if they knew you until I found Lloyd at that convenience store. It all boiled down to luck. I figured I'd still be looking for you at this point, really, or in all honesty, that I wouldn't have found anything and given up. You didn't really give me too many clues. With no address and no phone number, I was starting to think you didn't exist."

Vincent laughed. "So, now that you found me, what's next?" He finished placing ham on top a layer of mayonnaise on the bread.

"You were the missing piece to the puzzle. The most uncertain part about all of this is answered, in a way. Now I've got a way to learn about my parents, something I never had before. And I've realized there's so much I want to know about them and so little time to do it. I'd love to come back and stay for longer. I mean, of course if you're willing to have me as a guest. I don't want to bother you with all kinds of questions about them."

"Of course you can stay with me anytime you want. You won't ever be a bother, Sam, especially if you talking with me about your parents. I been waiting for this day for a long time, trust me. Been waiting to see what you looked like all grown up." Vincent rummaged around the ice chest. "You like pickles?"

"Sure, that's fine."

"Well, what about tomorrow? What you want to do? My schedule is wide open." Vincent opened the pickle jar and took two out.

"I'd like to visit the houseboat again, and maybe see some more of the Atchafalaya if we have the time."

Vincent slid the paper towel to Sam with the sandwich and pickle slice on top. "I tell you what, before you leave tomorrow, ole Vin is gonna give you all you can handle of the Basin."

"I like that idea."

Vincent took a bite of his sandwich then quickly crunched into the pickle. "So, if you didn't find me or found out I was dead or something, then what?" he mumbled with a mouthful.

"I thought about that. Guess it was a risk I was willing to take. I had nothing to lose. I would've gone back home and probably tried to think of another way to find out about them, and I guess you would have forever been a mystery."

"I know you got plenty of questions about your parents, but I don't know nothing about you yet. Vin's a little curious. So what do you do in Boston, anyway?"

Sam gave a tiny smile, trying to hide his displeasure about talking about home. It had been nice to not think about Boston for a while. But he couldn't expect to ask so many questions of his own and not receive any in return. "I work the graveyard shift at a shipyard."

"And?"

"And, what? That's it."

"Not married, no kids? Where you live?"

"No, never married, no girlfriend, and no kids. I don't think I would be able to afford them anyway. I barely could afford to come down here. And I live not far from down-town Boston. Close to the harbor where I work."

Vincent chewed on his sandwich and looked up at Sam with a steady gaze. It made Sam feel fidgety, as if Vincent was looking right through his casual responses and seeing deeper.

"You like what you do over there?" the old man asked.

"Eh, it's not so bad most days," Sam slurred, his mouth overflowing with food.

"You ain't got to lie to Vin, now. You not sounding very enthusiastic talking about this."

"There's nothing to tell. I've been on my own for a while and working that job. I like it that way." Sam hated lying to the old man, but he didn't feel it was his place to fill Vincent with guilt. He figured if he disclosed everything—about his struggles, about Nathan—it would only hurt the old man.

"I hear you. I'm like that in some ways," Vincent said. "Of course, I don't choose to be alone these days. I liked it more when I was younger."

Vincent finished up the last bite of his sandwich and wiped his mouth, while Sam finished the last of his pickle. Sam got up and threw away his trash in a nearby garbage can, then glanced over at Chris, who hadn't moved since falling back asleep. "Is he going to be OK?"

"Chris? Oh, yeah. He gets like that sometimes. He'll be fine."

Sam sat down and faced Vincent. The old man reclined back on the sofa, propping his feet up on the small table they both sat around.

"Thanks for taking me out to my parents' place. It meant a lot to see it." Sam took a few moments to put his thoughts into words. Now that he'd seen the Basin, he knew there was more to know about his parents than he first thought. "Obviously, I want to know about them—who they were, what they were like. But, especially now that I'm here, I want to know about the culture they lived in. I've missed out on knowing the Cajun culture I came from my whole life."

"You only human, Sam. It's what we all want to understand. We want to know we come from somewhere, we want to explain where we've been and how we got to where we are. I can understand that."

Vincent fit the mold of a typical, old Cajun man with his accent and rough appearance. Underneath that exterior, though, he clearly was an intelligent man; Sam could easily recognize that. And he saw a lot of himself in the old man.

Sam nodded, leaning forward on his stool. "That longing to know who I am and who they were increased tenfold when you brought me to that houseboat. That's one of the last things I expected to happen on this trip."

"I didn't mean to catch you off guard or anything."

"No, not at all, Vin. That's not what happened. I don't know if there could've been a better way for me to learn about my parents. I'm already looking forward to getting back there tomorrow. It was perfect."

"Good."

Sam joined Vincent on the sofa, took off his white sneakers, and kicked his feet up on the table. He turned his head toward Vincent. "They sound like they were both great people, just from hearing how you talk about them."

"They were the best. Ryan never backed down from nothing. But he wasn't stubborn. He knew when to ask for help. He wasn't hard headed like ole Vin. And Martha, she would've given the clothes off her back for anyone who needed them. They both would have. Martha was one of the most giving people on the planet, I'm telling you. They sure were some good people."

"I like hearing that. I like knowing that's the kind of people I came from."

"You missing that in your life, Sam?"

"Honestly, yeah. I've never had much of a good family in my life." He knew he shouldn't have said that. He crumpled his napkin in his hand, wishing he could take back the words. But he couldn't help it. It came natural through the warming way Vincent talked with him.

Before he could change the subject, Vincent responded. "How was Nathan and Evelyn? Were they good people?"

Sam tossed his napkin at the trashcan, and it went in, settling down with the other garbage, out of sight. And that's just how he wanted to keep his past. "That's a discussion for another night, Vin. Perhaps some other time."

Five

Sam abruptly opened his eyes and picked up his head. He looked around dazed, forgetting where he was for an instant. The first rays of the sun were jetting through the trees and into Chris' muggy cabin. The warm, late-summer air had crept in through the cracks and crevices. Sam uncurled the damp blanket from his lower half and looked over at Vincent and Chris, both of them still sound asleep. He decided he would get up to catch a glimpse of a Louisiana sunrise. He inched out of bed, tiptoeing across the room, careful not to make a sound even though he felt Vincent and Chris could sleep through anything, between the old man's snoring and the copious amount of alcohol Chris consumed the night before.

He walked down the stairs from the raised camp toward the dock. The farther he went out over the water on the pier, the grander his view became. He walked until he reached the end, and from there he had a stunning view of Grand Lake, one he couldn't get the night before from just moonlight. As he looked to his left and right, it seemed like the water didn't end, with a view that extended all the way north and south down the skinny lake. It stretched on for what looked like

miles and was bordered by trees of all sorts. He thought the
best part was that the dock faced directly east, giving him a
front row seat to the sunrise.

He sat down on the weathered boards of the pier, dangling his legs over the edge and letting his feet hang in the
cool water. Near the pier the water was brown, but farther
out the sun reflected off its surface and the lake glistened
with an amber hue. The red glow of the sun was subtle at
first, but minute by minute, the color grew more handsomely
bright. It consumed the trees and the sky, making it difficult
for Sam to discern where the water stopped and the sky began, morphing into a stunning display.

As he breathed slowly and the sun danced on his face,
Sam felt as if it was brightening his soul. It made him think
of his parents. He thought about how they once cruised the
same bayous he visited the day before, how perhaps they
fished the very lake he sat beside. The idea brought him an
immense sense of comfort. Growing up, he had only their
two names. But suddenly, in only a day, he had the houseboat, the paintings, and the photographs. His parents were
no longer a part of his imagination, characters he only saw in
his dreams. He could imagine them as they really looked, living out their lives in the Atchafalaya, with Vincent close by.

Sam was beginning to feel he had found some sense of
family in Vincent. Sure, he was still practically a stranger, but
Sam couldn't deny how the old man's warm welcome and
comforting personality made him feel. He had spent his life
without knowing what it felt like to have a family. The idea
was foreign to him, something he thought slipped away long
ago in his childhood. But over the course of one day, Vincent
showed him otherwise. He knew he had found something

special in the old man, even if he couldn't quite put his finger on it yet.

Sam opened his eyes, fully aware of the way his mind and body seemed in tune with his surroundings. He had never felt this way any place before. He was starting to understand why his parents picked the wilderness of the Atchafalaya for their home. But despite the powerful thoughts that rose up in him, at the same time those feelings were fleeting. He knew in just mere hours he'd be so far from this spot that it would seem like he was never even there. The thought made him cling deeper to the moment, as if to really ingrain the experience, like he would be able to unpack it later whenever he needed it, when he returned to Boston—and to the life he no longer wanted.

The thought crossed his mind that maybe Vincent was right: he belonged in Louisiana.

Noises coming from the camp behind him interrupted his reflection. He turned to see Vincent stumbling onto the porch. He hobbled down the creaking stairs and across the dock, holding a cup of coffee in each hand. "I had forgot my boots over here," he said, raising a leg and shaking his soiled, white rubber boot in the air. He continued walking toward Sam. "Man, these ole bones sure do some creaking and cracking early in the morning. Pretty, ain't it?" Vincent yawned and stretched his arms into the air above his head.

"It sure is."

"Now, all Vin needs is a smoke and we good to go, young man. Here, I got you some coffee."

Sam grabbed the white, foam cup from Vincent. "Back to Riley Bayou?"

"Oh, don't you worry, we going back. First I'm gonna

catch us some breakfast. Well, shall I say we gonna catch it?"

"Like, what, hunting?"

"No, no, no—we gonna go fishing, boy. We'll see if some of your daddy rubbed off on you. You ever been?"

"Yeah, once."

"Only once?"

"That's right," Sam said with a touch of embarrassment. "I've been with a coworker before. We didn't have any luck."

"That's why you didn't catch anything. It ain't about luck. It's about knowing exactly where the fish are and why. Fishing is about more than throwing out a line and hoping."

Vincent revved up his boat motor and the vessel shot off, carrying him and Sam away from the island and into the vast expanse of Grand Lake. He powered his motor faster until he found a cruising speed. In one hand he held coffee, the other rested on the tiller handle to steer the boat, and in his mouth he shifted around a cigarette. The old man puffed it, then grabbed it between two free fingers around his cup, and took a sip of coffee.

"We not going far from Riley Bayou," Vincent shouted above the whining of the outboard motor as smoke escaped his mouth. "There's a little secret spot I know of near Catfish Lake where we can catch some bream two times bigger than the size of my hand."

Though Sam didn't have the slightest idea what a bream was, he gave a thumbs up and smiled, showing he was up for the challenge.

After snaking through a few more bayous, Vincent slowed down as he and Sam neared a dead-end canal with a section of cypress trees spaced out just enough for the boat to slip through. The old Cajun motored slowly through a few of the trees before killing the engine. "OK, this is it. Now, I'm gonna bait up the first one but you gotta do the next."

Vincent picked up a fishing pole from the floor of his boat. He reached into an ice chest devoid of ice, but full of grimy water, and pulled out a cracked plastic container. His yellow fingernails popped open the blue, round top and dipped inside into the dirt that filled it. He rummaged around and picked out a worm.

"Now, you stick the hook through the head, then out the back and wrap it around the hook once. Then you stick the hook through it again," Vincent instructed as he stuck a worm on a small hook, looking up to make sure Sam understood. "Got it?"

Sam had watched carefully as Vincent finagled the squirming worm onto the hook. He wasn't squeamish, but was surprised by how the old man stuck the slimy creature on there so well. He wondered if he could recreate the practice so skillfully.

"I think so," he said.

"Well, go ahead and cast next to any of these trees. When the cork goes under, pull up and set the hook. Then reel that sucker in."

Sam looked at the reel in his hand, a black and silver contraption he wasn't entirely sure how to use. He clicked the black button on the reel face, which he discovered let out the line. He held the button again and casted near the first cypress that caught his eye. To his surprise, the hook didn't land in the nearby trees, but dropped safely a few yards in front of him in the water.

"Well, well, well, look at that," Vincent said, shaking his head. "You ain't half bad."

"Beginners luck, maybe?" As soon as the words left Sam's mouth, his orange cork submerged.

"Pull up, boy. Pull that thing up!" Vincent shouted in excitement.

Sam frantically followed Vincent's directions, pulling his rod up toward his head. He felt a pressure on the end of his pole. The clear, thin line zigzagged in the water back and forth.

"Reel!" Vincent shouted from the back of the boat.

Sam firmed up his grasp on the handle of the fishing pole and reeled in the fish. He did so until the cork slammed against the rod tip, a small fish flopping around in the air not far behind.

"You reeled too much. Here, bring it into the boat," Vincent said as he laughed.

Sam plopped the fish onto the floor of the boat. It jumped and wriggled about at his feet. "Is it a bream?"

Vincent looked down at the small, olive drab creature that most everyone outside of Louisiana called a bluegill. "Yep, and a nice one, too. Take it off the hook and throw it in this little ice chest, then cast back again. It looks like we gonna catch good this morning."

After about an hour of steady catching, Vincent's ice chest was full with fifteen bream. The old man sounded jubilant as he inspected the morning's catch. "We did good, I tell you. That's plenty for breakfast."

"I'd say so. Just in time, too. I'm hungry."

"Remember, now, that catching is half the part. Now comes the real fun. We gonna go clean them."

Vincent cranked up his outboard and a plume of smoke erupted from its exhaust. Sam looked at it with concern, but

Vincent didn't seem to notice and carefully maneuvered through the cypress and back into the canal he and Sam had come from earlier.

Before long, they were back near Riley Bayou, cruising down the straight canal leading up to its entrance. Vincent motored up to the old houseboat and moored near the side facing the nearest bank, giving the two men a view of the trees and shrubbery lining the bayou. Sam stepped onto the porch and turned back to see Vincent right behind him with the ice chest in both hands and a tiny barbeque pit sitting on top of it. The old man seemed to struggle to get out of the skiff. His arms shook and he was getting winded trying to simultaneously step out of the boat while he hauled the load. It worried Sam enough that he stretched his hands out to take the ice chest. "Let me give you a hand with that, Vin."

"Don't even think about it. The day I can't carry stuff out my boat is the day I'm gonna die."

Sam shrugged and cleared the way for Vincent. He figured that years of living alone in the Atchafalaya had given the old man an intensely independent personality. Even though he hadn't seen Vincent slow down yet, the episode worried him. The thought crossed his mind that if he didn't come back to Louisiana soon, Vincent might not be there to visit. Maybe he'd lose him almost as soon as he found him. Sam shook his head slightly, ridding himself of the negative thoughts. He watched as Vincent managed to climb out of the boat and onto the porch in one piece. It gave him some assurance that maybe he was just over thinking the situation.

Vincent kneeled and laid everything he held on the floor: an ice chest, barbeque pit, bag of charcoal, a bowl, a skillet, and a knife. All of the contents, minus the ice chest, fit neatly inside the miniature pit.

"Where'd that barbeque pit come from, anyway?" Sam asked as he took a knee near Vincent.

"I keep it under my milk crate—fits perfectly."

"Do you use it that much?"

"Oh, yeah. You never know when you gonna want to eat some breakfast or supper." Vincent looked toward the wooded area just beyond where they were on the porch and pointed to a section of land. "That's where your momma had her garden. The area is almost unrecognizable now, but thirty years ago, it was full of green beans, bell peppers, eggplant or whatever Martha could get her hands on."

Vincent plucked a fish out of the ice chest, grabbed the knife, and quickly got to work on prepping breakfast. He narrated his every move to Sam who squatted nearby, his words coming as fast as his hands were moving. He scraped off the scales with the knife, cut the head off, slit up the belly, and pulled the innards out. Then he was off to the next one.

Sam just looked on as Vincent's aged hands delicately carved each fish with surgical precision. Almost as soon as Vincent had started, the fish lay in the bowl and were ready to stick on the lit barbeque pit. Vincent plopped as many of the bream as he could onto the cast iron pan. He closed the lid to the pit and then sat back against one of the structural support posts of the porch. He pointed to a jumble of logs near the bank. "Look over there. That's the log pile your daddy used to make all his pirogues. It's like a Cajun canoe. We'd go look for cypress that had sunk a long time ago. He'd dive head first into the bayou and find them big ole things. We'd bring as many as we could back here. Then he'd cut them by hand to make them."

"So he was pretty handy?"

"Oh, yeah. Like I said, he was a fast learner," Vincent said as he prepared another cigarette, taking tobacco from a little pack and wrapping it up into white paper.

"Did you teach him?"

"He learned in less than a month. Took me almost a half a year to even learn how to make my first crude one, and then it didn't even float. That boy there made one worthy of selling on his first go round."

"Think you could teach me one day?"

Vincent licked the cigarette, finished rolling it, and stuck it in his mouth. "Well, I don't see why not." He struck a match on the wooden floor of the houseboat and lit the cigarette, smoke rising above his face. "All we would need would be a few good pieces of wood and a few weeks, and I could get you making some."

Vincent opened the lid to the barbeque pit. "Looks like this first batch is done." He scooped the meat onto a piece of tinfoil that was resting on the top of the closed ice chest. Then he took the rest of the bream from the bowl and laid them on another fresh bed of sizzling oil.

"But you don't have very long here," Vincent said as he closed the lid of the pit.

"Right. I'm not looking forward to leaving this afternoon and going back to Boston." The beauty of the morning had already started to fade in Sam's mind, just as he hoped it wouldn't. He thought about how it would soon be replaced with the sea of buildings and noisy highways in Boston. He pushed away the dreary thoughts, determined to enjoy this slice of paradise while he could.

"Cypress trees and bayous sure are a lot prettier than

some ole, big city. Now that you've come here and seen all this, you think you'll be coming back again soon?" Vincent asked.

"I definitely want to, Vin. I haven't had much time to process any of this, though, and there's still so much I want to know about Mom and Dad." It was the first time Sam had referred to Ryan and Martha that way, at least out loud. He stopped before finishing his thought and smiled. It came out natural, and he liked that. "So, I'm pretty sure I'll be back soon to learn more."

After Sam and Vincent finished breakfast, they cleaned up and walked inside the home. The only thing from the scene that had changed from the evening before was more light made it through the windows. If anything, it made the place only look dirtier. Sam walked to an overturned stool near the table and picked it upright. He checked its stability then sat on it.

Vincent leaned against the cabinets near the sink. "I tell you what, ole Vin was born not far from here and I've barely ever been outside of Louisiana. When I have left, I always couldn't wait to get back. And still, I surely do love this place."

"I wish I knew how that felt. I know it's only been a day, but this place just beckons."

"The Atchafalaya has a way of doing that to you. It got in your parents' blood. That's how it works. Once it's in your blood, it sticks."

"Just being in this house is comforting, knowing they both were here all those years ago. It's like they're here with me right now. Like I can feel their presence inside this place."

"I used to come spend a lot of time here after they passed. I'd sit down and just stare out the window. I swear I could still hear your momma laughing after hearing a joke from Ryan. People say places are haunted. I agree. By ghosts? Nah, not by ghosts. By the memories of the people you loved that you hold in your head." Vincent paused and looked at Sam. "This place will forever haunt me. I can feel them here, too. Always have. It makes it a lot easier having you here. Seems like I got both of them standing right in front of me."

Sam smiled. The stack of boxes in the corner of the room caught his eye. "Oh, I need to check in these boxes."

He made his way to the two cardboard boxes stacked one on top of the other in the corner near the bedroom door. When he opened the first he found some old clothes: a pair of overalls, a few shirts, and a torn dress. "Was this theirs?"

Deep wrinkles formed around Vincent's forehead as he squinted his eyes. "Yep, pretty sure."

Sam rubbed the clothes. The fibers were fragile and looked as if they'd rip with ease. He placed them to the side and opened the next box in the stack. He instantly smiled as he uncovered the contents. "It's all paintings!"

Though the heat had damaged many of them, the images were still mostly visible. Sam recognized the first on the pile as a portrait of Ryan. "Look at this, Vin. This is awesome," Sam said with a grin.

There were eight in all, including the portrait of Ryan. Most of them were scenes of the Atchafalaya—sunsets, sunrises, animals, or trees. The last in the pile was a fleur-de-lis that bared the words *'famille, amour, une vie.'*

"What's this mean?" Sam asked as he held up the picture for Vincent to see, pointing at the foreign words.

Vincent rubbed his ruffled beard and he smiled. "Been a long time since I seen that. It's French. It means family, love, one life. It's something your momma made up. She would say it all the time."

Sam looked back at the phrase. "That's beautiful."

The words wrapped around the ancient French symbol in a circle. The background was orange, the fleur-de-lis black, and the words white.

"She'd wrap you up in your crib, lay you down, and whisper it to you," Vincent said. "It meant a lot to have you, you know. She loved her family. Loved you."

Sam loaded the other paintings back into the box, but kept the fleur-de-lis out and hung it on an exposed nail on the wall.

Vincent kept looking at the painting, beaming. Then he scanned the interior of the houseboat. "I been saying for years I should fix up this ole thing. But I'm afraid it's too far gone now. As much as I would hate to, I been wanting to at least take what's left and bring it back to my house. If I don't, this place will sink and we'll lose everything."

"Yeah, we'll have to do that, Vin."

"So that means you have to come back if you gonna be helping."

Sam smiled over at Vincent. "That's right."

"I been thinking about it, and I wanted to let you know, my door is always open for you. If you ever get sick of Boston and want to come and stay with ole Vin as long as you want, you don't have to write or try to get in touch with me. Just come. You family, and family is always welcome."

It was as if Vincent saw through him, like the old man knew exactly what to say, and when to say it. Sam wished he could've lunged forward, hugged Vincent and told him he'd move in the next day. But he didn't think it was a realistic option. He turned and faced Vincent, then walked back to the stool and sat on it.

"That's awfully kind of you to offer that." Sam replied more timidly than he actually felt. He wasn't accustomed to feelings like this, nor did he really know how to outwardly express himself as vibrantly as he wanted to.

As Sam and Vincent left the battered houseboat so Sam could catch his flight in New Orleans, he looked back into the interior one last time while Vincent continued onto the boat. The bright orange painting caught his eye before he stepped onto the porch. He lightly rubbed his hand on the faded exterior wall, perhaps in an attempt to put a physical connection to what he felt, as if to ensure something tangible in his memory, other than just the recollections Vincent had relayed to him.

Sam joined Vincent in the boat and pushed it away from the porch. He looked at the old, sinking structure and smiled as he drifted farther from it. Vincent drove through the maze of bayous and lakes as he and Sam made their way out of the Atchafalaya back toward the boat landing. Just like the day before, the birds hung in the sky as they flew from tree to tree. Sam looked up at them and knew that he was going to miss the Basin. He hoped he would return one day to the Atchafalaya.

Six

Sam tried to push the distant lights and activity that surrounded him out of his mind and imagine the scene he experienced on Grand Lake. It had been just under three weeks since he landed in Boston and continued his late-night job at the shipyard, but he was still finding it hard to get back to his routine. Towering cranes repetitively plucked colorful rectangular shipping containers from the decks of the ships, while pickup trucks, forklifts, and eighteen-wheelers crisscrossed in every direction. But Sam made all of the lights disappear; he blocked out the noises as he imagined cypress trees in the distance. He remembered the way watching the sunrise on the pier in Louisiana made him feel and the peaceful ambiance of the morning. He reached deep inside his mind to try to mimic the image as he remembered it. In this pensive moment he smiled and breathed deep as he had that morning back in Louisiana.

"Sam! Hey, Sam! What the hell are you doing?" barked Dee, Sam's boss, as he poked his bald head around the corner of a set of industrial storage containers. "Those units were supposed to get to St. Louis. You've got them loaded on the wrong truck going all the way to California!"

"Oh, sorry, Dee," Sam said before frantically jotting down a few figures. "I got it. I'm making the correction. Todd is on it."

"What the hell are you looking at?" Dee grumbled as he started back to his office, his thin lips pursed and his brawny, Neanderthal-like frame stomping arrogantly through the dock. "Shake a leg. We got an hour before crew change."

"Got it."

Sam walked back to the receiving area and prepared to record the corrected shipment number. He was thankful he hadn't gotten more of a dressing down from Dee, who was notorious for being unnecessarily tough, which didn't make him well liked among the crews.

"Better keep your mind from wandering again. Dee will likely lose it if he catches you daydreaming another time," Todd, one of Sam's co-workers said, as he pulled up alongside Sam in a forklift.

"I know," Sam said, trying to catch up with his writing.

Todd took off with a pallet full of supplies down the dock leaving Sam alone with his thoughts. He attempted to keep them at bay and focus on his work, but it was of no use. He glanced back out across the bay and longed for Louisiana.

"Dude, are you just standing there?" Todd passed by again, and Sam realized he was standing in the same spot from a few minutes ago. "Dee is going to blow his lid. Let's go!"

Instead of scrambling to get back to work, Sam looked up at Todd and said, "What's the point?" He realized that this night had been just like the one before, and that tomorrow would be the same. As the distant blast of a ship's horn sounded and forklifts darted back and forth across the dock, Sam realized none of it mattered, at least not for him. He set down his clipboard and headed for Dee's office ignoring Todd as he shouted, "Where are you going now?"

Before he could get to the office, Todd grabbed him by the shoulder and turned him around. "What's with you?"

"I've had it," Sam snapped. "I'm done with this, with the job, with Boston, with Dee!"

Todd shook his head. "You're quitting?" His tone was less confrontational and more confused.

"I am, and you know what, maybe this job and this life is OK for you. You've got a family, children, a wife; you've got something to keep you going every night. I don't have a damn thing." Sam stopped, knowing he was being too tough on Todd, who he considered one of his only friends in Boston. He immediately regretted his outburst. "I'm sorry. It's not you. It's just this. Everything here. I didn't mean to snap at you."

Todd shook his head and puckered his brows slightly. "Do what you need to do. But at least finish the shift first."

"I am, but I've got to do this right now, Todd. If I don't, I may never have the courage to do it again. I'll be back in a second." Sam turned and entered the tin building where Dee's office was housed. He was certain that Dee wouldn't take well to an interruption, especially one that resulted in one less employee, but Sam knew he had to tell him—before he lost the sense of clarity that was telling him this was the right move.

"Miller, why aren't you working?" Dee shouted as soon as Sam stepped inside.

"You got a second?"

"Half a second."

Sam walked into the dimly lit office and sat down in front of Dee's desk, which was strewn with papers and ashes from cigarettes. Dee was focused on reading an inventory report that Sam and the other crews produced every morning for his approval. Smoke from his cigarette floated up around his face, occasionally visible as it rose through the sparse light from the lamp on his desk.

"Well, what do you want?" Dee said without looking up from the report.

"I wanted to tell you that it's been a pleasure working with you all these years," Sam said, which caused Dee to look up with his eyebrows furrowing.

"Sure, it's been great. Now spit out what you came here to tell me."

Sam paused and took a breath, his leg bouncing slightly. "I'm giving you my two weeks' notice."

"Two weeks' notice?" Dee had a perturbed expression on his face.

"Yeah."

"Where the hell are you going?"

"I'm moving to Louisiana."

"For what?" Dee said after a short pause.

"Well, I'm going to live there; thinking about trying my hand at being a fisherman."

Dee snorted. "You're not cut out for that. Too weak. I've known that since you showed up here begging for a job. It's why for almost ten years all you've done is jot numbers down all night. I leave the heavy lifting to the real men."

Sam's hands clenched into fists as they rested on his thighs. He bit his lip to avoid snapping back.

"You know this is a busy time of year for us," Dee continued. "And after the cuts I've had to make having one less man around is going to be hell. Not to mention that I didn't cut you, and now you're quitting?"

"Yep," Sam responded calmly. While he wanted to stand up and tell Dee how he really felt—that he could take his lousy job and go to hell—he held it in. At that point, he figured any pleasure he'd get out of telling Dee off would quickly dissipate. Besides, he preferred the satisfaction he'd get out of knowing that Dee hadn't gotten the better of him.

"Pack up your shit today," Dee growled, appearing to hold in his frustration. "Forget about the two weeks. And forget about your pay for tonight, too."

A few more words from Dee and Sam thought maybe he wouldn't be able to keep his cool after all. "I was going to finish my shift through the morning. I just wanted to tell you now," Sam protested.

"Fine, you'll get half your pay then. You might as well get the hell out of here while that's still how I want to handle it. Tell Stacie to print out the release form, sign it, and get on your way."

Sam stood up with his fists still clenched, and his face red and hot as he stared at Dee. He could feel himself start to lose whatever calm he had been trying to hold onto.

Dee looked up from the report and squinted his eyes. "You got something you want to say?" He stood and broadened his shoulders.

At that point, all Sam wanted was to spring forward and sock Dee good a few times. But he opted for the less showy response. "You're a real ass, you know that?"

Dee's eyes widened and his expression registered complete shock at Sam's response. But he recovered quickly. "Get the hell out of my office. And I don't want to see your face in here again."

Sam nodded and walked out.

After signing the release form, what irritation Sam felt floated away as he walked out of the office, replaced by an immense sense of relief. It felt good to finally tell Dee off, something all the crew members probably wished they could do. Any doubts about moving to Louisiana quickly faded away. He was glad he wouldn't have to put up with people like Dee anymore. More and more, he was seeing Louisiana as a fresh start. He saw bayou country as a place where he could forget his failures and frustrations, leaving it all behind in Boston. He vowed in that moment, staring at the cranes and scurrying activity in the distance of the shipyard, that he would always be thankful for the opportunity to start life again.

Seven

When Sam's Greyhound bus rumbled into New Orleans, he wasn't nervous like he was during his initial trip. He knew exactly where he was headed and he couldn't wait to get there. After grabbing his backpack and duffle bag from the overhead luggage rack, he stepped outside into the muggy Louisiana afternoon with a grin. There was something about the way the humid air engulfed him and filled his lungs that was both distinct and overpowering. He thought, in a way, it felt like he had never left.

Sam stood just outside the automatic doors of the bus station and looked for the shuttle that would take him to Bayou Pigeon. To his right he spotted it, waiting on him in a line of other cars. The cream-colored sedan was exactly as the driver described it to him. He was lucky to have found the man. Most of the shuttle services in the New Orleans area didn't ferry as far as he wanted to go. The gentleman next to the car was the only person who agreed to drive two hours northwest. He was a middle-aged man, heavy set and with a bushy, brown mustache. He wore blue jean shorts, white shoes with two Velcro straps, and a gray collared shirt that was damp with sweat from the midday sun. As Sam walked up to him, the man stopped leaning against the four-door sedan and stood straight.

"Sam?" the driver said.

"That's me. I hope you weren't waiting out here for too long."

"Nah, just a few minutes. Here, let me help you with those." The driver muscled Sam's bags into the trunk of the car with haste. It appeared that he wanted nothing more than to be in his vehicle with the air conditioning cranked up. "Alright, sir, climb aboard."

Sam slid into the passenger's seat and noticed a rosary hanging from the rear view mirror. Other than that, the car was devoid of decorations; it was also spotless, which was quite the opposite from what he had come to expect with cabs in Boston.

"It's Mike, right?" Sam asked.

Mike nodded. He took out a sheet of paper that was neatly tucked in the middle console. He began to read from it. "So, you're going to Bayou Pigeon. It's about two hours from here northwest. And I quoted you $100 for the trip. Sound right?"

"That's it."

"OK, let's get going then."

Mike shifted into drive and took off. He relaxed back in his seat like it was a recliner and drove with casualness. Sam glanced down to watch Mike use both feet on the pedals, even though the car was an automatic. Mike's right shoe pressed down on the gas while his left sat cocked until he needed to hit the break.

"I've never heard of Bayou Pigeon before. I had to look it up when you called to figure out where it was," Mike said.

"It's a pretty small place. I wouldn't call it a town or even a village. It's more of an unincorporated community of sorts."

"You live there or something?"

"Well, not now, I don't. But I will in just a few short hours."

"Ah, I see. So you're moving there."

"That's right."

Mike merged onto the interstate that shot out of the New Orleans metro area. The road crossed a concrete levee where on one side was a sprawling metropolis, and on the other a swamp. Sam looked behind him and saw nothing but concrete and buildings spanning for miles. He turned back around and gazed out ahead of the vehicle. His only view, aside from the road, was of swamp and marsh. New Orleans truly was smack in the middle of a swamp, Sam thought as he peered out the window between a lull in the conversation with Mike. As Mike motored the sedan across the bridge that traversed the levee, Sam understood why it was so easy for the place to flood.

"So, what's bringing you to Bayou Pigeon?" Mike said after a few moments of silence.

Sam was looking out the window, preoccupied with his thoughts, then turned to look at Mike. He figured he'd never see the guy again, so why not indulge him? So he told him nearly everything. He talked about Vincent, his previous trip to Louisiana, his parents, and leaving Boston.

Mike seemed to hang on every word.

By the time Sam reached the end of the story, he and Mike were surrounded by cypress trees casting shadows over the car, nearing Vincent's battered driveway.

"And that's what pretty much led me to here," Sam said, wrapping up the story. "Looks like I finished that up just in time, too. I think the turn is coming up. It's hard to find."

"Yeah, no problem. Just let me know when you see it, and I'll slow down a bit."

Sam wasn't exactly sure where Vincent's road was exactly, but he knew it shouldn't be much farther from where they were.

"There it is," Sam said as he whipped his head back, pointing to what he thought looked like the entrance. "Sorry, we passed it up."

"That's alright. Ain't nobody coming. I'll just put her in reverse."

"I should warn you, this road we're about to go down isn't in the best shape. You may want to take it easy."

"I won't get stuck, will I?" Mike said after reversing and putting his car into drive.

Sam rolled down the window and stuck his head out to get a better look. "I'm not sure."

Mike pulled into the edge of the pathway, squinted his eyes as he looked at the mud and water and shook his head. "I can't take you down there, sorry. I can't risk getting stranded out in the middle of nowhere. Got some more fares today."

"Hey, I understand, Mike. I wouldn't want you to get stranded out here, either."

"Well, alright, sir. I'll get your bags out," Mike said after unbuckling the seatbelt and opening his door. He got out and headed to the trunk.

Sam took out a $100 bill from his wallet and met Mike toward the rear of the car.

"Thanks, Mike, I got it from here. Here you go." Sam handed Mike the fare and then picked up his two bags.

Mike closed the trunk. "Great, well thanks for riding and good luck with everything. I've got to tell you, I've heard a lot of stories over the years, and yours is one of the few I won't forget. It's by far one of the most interesting stories I've had the pleasure of hearing. If you ever need a ride anywhere around New Orleans, you have my number."

"Absolutely. But I have a feeling I won't be making it to the city anytime soon."

Mike reversed the car back onto the gravel, and shouted out of his window, "I hope everything goes well for you down here. I gotta say, I admire someone who can pick up and do what you're doing. Good luck." Then he shot off, leaving Sam alone on the muddy driveway.

Sam trudged through the dirt and mud, taking care not to step into a pothole and soak his shoes. But just a few steps in and he drenched his right leg up to his mid-calf.

Well, that didn't last long, he thought.

He continued slogging through the mud as what felt like rivers of sweat ran down his back. The heat was harsher than he remembered. Mosquitoes buzzed around his ears, and probed his soaked arms and neck for a quick feast. Instead of losing his cool, Sam was happy to be walking toward his new home. He continued proudly like a long-lost son returning after years of absence. He couldn't wait to see the look on Vincent's face when the old man saw he was back. The thought made him smile.

But the smile soon faded when the old shack came into view. Sam didn't see Vincent's truck nearby. The boat was gone, too. He wondered if Vincent had gone out into the

Basin for the day. He glanced down at his muddy shoes and legs. It wasn't the triumphal return he was expecting: alone and getting tormented by mosquitoes.

Sam walked up the creaking stairs of Vincent's house and placed his bags on the front porch. He checked the door to see if it was locked. It wasn't. He kicked off his muddy shoes and socks, took his bags in, walked out to the porch, and sat on a swing. It appeared to be a new addition to the house, and thus looked out of place. Instead of being gray like the rest of the home, the wood was yellow and looked to be freshly cut. Sam rubbed his hand on one of the silver, shiny chains that secured it to the rafters above his head.

Sam figured he'd just wait on the swing for the old man to return. It was nearly 6 p.m. With a little more than two hours of daylight left, Sam thought Vincent would be showing up anytime. If the old Cajun had a phone it would've been easier to relay a message, but Sam didn't mind waiting outside alone for a spell. It was an opportunity to think some more about what he wanted to do with his new life in Louisiana. This feeling was new for him. For most of his life, he didn't think about the future because it wasn't something that brought him comfort. He never could afford to get an education and he didn't have the time even if he had wanted to try. His job demanded most of his free time and the subpar pay meant he couldn't do much when he wasn't at work. For so long, it seemed as if he was trapped in a cycle of making just enough money to pay bills and rent, a circle he never seemed to be able to escape.

He kicked his feet to push the swing back, hoping the movement would keep a few of the mosquitoes away. It didn't help much. As he rocked back and forth, he peered at the dense Louisiana swampland. He knew that money wouldn't be much of an issue anymore, especially since Vincent had told him of the value in bartering. He didn't have to pay rent, worry about bills or spend his nights out on the Boston harbor. He was going to be a Louisiana fisherman—just like his parents. It was a new beginning, the clean slate he had always hoped to find. That's what the Atchafalaya provided, Sam thought: an accepting way of life and a fresh start. It seemed that people didn't need much education to excel, and social class, race, sex, and ethnicity didn't matter. The Atchafalaya treated everyone the same. All someone needed to do was work hard and something could be made out of life. Under its formidable first appearance, under all the eerie trees and murky swamp water, Sam thought it was one of the most welcoming places he had ever been.

Despite the occasional mosquito buzzing around his face, Sam stayed wrapped up in his thoughts until eventually he kicked back and fell asleep on the swing. Almost as soon he dozed off, the sound of a vehicle approaching woke him. He sat up, blinking his heavy eyes and yawning. As he suspected, it was Vincent in the old Ford. Ole Blue jolted up and down as it conquered all the potholes. Of course, Vincent's prized skiff bounced along in tow. Sam stood and walked to the porch steps, and waved.

Vincent glimpsed Sam and stuck his head out of the door's window. "Sammy boy!" he shouted.

Vincent parked and quickly made his way to the house, while Sam walked down from the porch to greet him.

Vincent grinned and gave Sam a hug. "That was quick," he said, wearing the same overalls and retro hat from the last time Sam saw him. "I'm glad I didn't have to wait twenty-five years before I got to see you again."

"What can I say? I guess this place got the better of me." Sam clapped Vincent's back, not wanting to let go of the old man.

Vincent pulled back and grabbed Sam's shoulders, giving them a squeeze as he examined his face. "Hot damn, boy, I'm glad you back. How long you staying this time?"

"As long as you'll have me."

"You staying for good?" Vincent's white eyebrows rose.

"That's right."

Vincent smiled again and laughed. "That's some good news. You made this ole man's day. But, you know what could make it even better?"

"What's that?"

"You help me clean these catfish I caught this afternoon so we can have supper." Vincent motioned to his truck.

Sam grabbed the bucket of fish from the back bed of the pickup. "And so it begins, my intro to bayou living. I feel like I've got a lot to learn."

Vincent laughed and led Sam to the backyard. "Oh, I hope you ready. Plop 'em on this table here." Vincent patted the top of a stainless steel table.

Sam lifted the bucket of catfish and placed it where Vincent indicated as he took a look around the yard. He hadn't been back here on his first visit. The old Cajun had three more boats stashed in the rear of his house. Next to the boats were wired crawfish and fish traps, a few hundred of them sitting in a jumble. Next to the traps was an antique pickup from the 50s, older and in worse shape than Ole Blue. It was rusted and clearly didn't run due to a missing engine and tires. Next to the truck was a pile of outboard motors laid on their side, three total. Waist-high grass and dense shrubbery consumed everything else in sight, until the land gave way to black water and cypress trees toward the rear of the property.

The old man took out the first catfish in the pile with one hand; in the other he held a filet knife. "Catfish got three barbs that'll prick you if you not careful," he instructed Sam as he used the knife to point them out. "The one on the back is the biggest, but that ain't the one you gotta worry about. The two on the sides by his head are smaller and will prick you just as much. Now, when they ain't alive, you fine. You ain't gotta worry about him wriggling about and sticking you. It's when they alive you gotta worry about them. Now, you just slip your hand behind all three of them and cut the head off."

Vincent went to work, gutting, skinning, and cutting up the first catfish, making sure Sam had a first-hand view of what to do. He talked fast, his garbled accent in full swing, so Sam had to be on high alert to keep up. In between the directions, Vincent would shoot questions at Sam about what made him return to Louisiana so soon, making understanding the directions a bit harder.

"So you staying as long as I'll let you, huh? What's your plan?" Vincent asked without looking up from the fish he worked on.

"For starters, learn how to live on the bayou, get to know my parents more, and maybe get to know myself."

"Seems like you got more of a plan this time."

"Well, I figured that if I quit my job I'd have to make certain I had some type of direction to take when I got here. I don't want to get in your way at all, though. So if I'm any kind of bother, I want you to let me know."

"Boy, you didn't get my hint before you left? I told you I wanted you to come back. You ain't gonna be in my way."

"I know, I know. I just had to make sure."

"So how'd you get out so quick, anyway?"

"I left everything, quit my job, gave away most of my stuff. I don't ever plan on going back. I haven't felt so much relief in years."

Vincent laughed, his eyes full of happiness. "That's good to hear. Well, you definitely gonna get a Cajun 101 course if you want to live on the bayou as a fisherman. We'll consider this your first unofficial lesson. Tomorrow we'll head to the Basin for the first day of getting you up to speed."

Vincent had raced through the first load of fish in no time, leaving a pile of innards and other remains in a trash bag and a stack of fresh, filleted meat in a glass bowl.

"Now, you seen me do it a couple times," Vincent said. "Go get the other load from the truck and you gonna do them. Best way to learn how to do something is to do it on your own."

Sam walked around to the front of the house and grabbed the remaining catfish and walked back to Vincent.

"You got it?" Vincent asked.

"We'll see."

Sam picked up a fish from the bucket, careful to avoid the barbs, and positioned his hands just as Vincent had showed him. But it didn't go exactly to plan.

"Ow!" Sam grabbed his right hand then shook it violently, as if to relieve some of the pain shooting down his fingers.

"It got you good? Let me see." Vincent looked at Sam's

hand. A small puncture wound dotted his index finger, blood slowly oozing out. "It's not that bad."

Sam winced but calmed. The cut had mostly startled him more than it hurt. "We'll just call this me earning my stripes. How about that?"

Vincent smiled. "Hey, I like the way that sounds. Got a good attitude, just like your daddy did."

With a small towel wrapped around his wound, Sam cut off the fish's head, cut down the middle of the belly, pulled the intestines out, and started skinning the leathery exterior of the fish. He had a bit of trouble but Vincent gave him encouragement—at least he avoided another tangle with the barbs.

"Look at you. Not too shabby," Vincent said as he looked on.

It took Sam a little longer than Vincent to prepare each fish. After he finished with the last, he laughed. "Not quite like yours."

While Vincent's fillets were one slab of smooth, slightly pink meat, Sam's had chunks missing and were cut into several slices.

"You got plenty of time to get better at cleaning fish. If you are like your momma and daddy, you'll learn fast." Vincent patted Sam on the back, then grabbed the bowl of fish. "Well, come on, let's go have some supper and visit."

The two men retired inside the shack where Sam sat near the kitchen table while Vincent heated up a cast iron skillet on the antique gas stove. He also started a pot of coffee, despite the waning sunlight. Vincent was particularly fond of coffee. He always found an excuse to slurp down a black cup: new visitors, old ones, and any afternoon conversations were fair game. It didn't seem to matter the time of day, either. The old man could ingest caffeine at any time and still get a full night's rest.

Vincent lathered the fish with spices and a few herbs. "It's been a long time since Vin had a roommate. When I was in the service was probably the last time."

"What branch did you serve?"

"Was in the army during Korea. I never went over to fight, lucky for me. I sat on a base in North Carolina until the war was over. But other than that, Vin's been by himself. Well, that was probably for the best when I lived on my houseboat. Oh man, that thing was small. Way smaller than the one your parents lived in. It had one room with the bed, a sink, and a table and chairs."

"No bathroom?"

"Had an outhouse on a little ridge next to where I moored it."

Vincent splashed some water onto the skillet. It sizzled and popped, a sign the skillet was hot enough. He then laid four of the catfish filets, covered with flour, on top of a bed of oil. The meat sizzled, filling the tiny house with an aroma that made Sam's stomach rumble.

Vincent left the fish frying to check on his coffee. "Good, looks like the coffee is ready, too. You want some?"

"No, thanks. I'll never be able to sleep tonight."

Vincent nodded as he poured the coffee into a white mug. He sat across the table from Sam and took a sip, steam billowing from the top of his cup. "We had our own little community on Riley Bayou. In addition to me and your parents, there was Gerald and Avia Babineaux, a fella named

Rusty Guidry—he owned this property here—and George and Linda Stelly. Your parents were probably younger by around thirty to fifty years compared to everyone there."

"Did everyone move out like you did?"

"George moved out when Linda died. But everyone else stayed until they died. Gerald was the last to go. He passed away in '91. I moved out, of course, right after I lost your parents in '88. It was hard living in the Basin at an older age. All the other houseboats got moved out, except your parents. Then, twenty-something years later, the bayou started silting up and all the trees started growing and blocked off the bayou because of that canal the damn oil company built through the area." Vincent took a giant gulp of coffee, stood up from the table, and walked over to the stove and inspected the skillet of fish. "Well, that looks about ready to eat."

"Do you need help, Vin?" Sam asked.

"No, no, sit down, I got it. And help yourself to a beer or whatever in the fridge."

Vincent laid the steaming hot, golden brown fish out on a piece of tin foil on his shoddy kitchen table. He garnished them with more cayenne pepper and a tablespoon of melted butter. It was clear where he got his potbelly from, especially after the old man cracked open a beer. "Alright well, dig in."

Sam had looked forward to getting to again eat the fresh fish Vincent cooked up. As he took the first bite, the freshness of the meat was again apparent, accentuated with a hint of Cajun spices. "This is some good fish."

"The only way I know how to make it. It would've been a little fresher if I would've got them over here faster. They sat in the boat for a little while."

"I'm sure it's easier to not have to travel back over here after fishing. Have you ever thought about moving back?"

"To the Basin?"

"Yeah."

"I have. But I'm realistic enough to know I can't. While I like to act like I don't skip a beat all the time, my body often says otherwise. It's a lot rougher living out there than it is out here with the protection of the levees. For starters, too, the next flood would be hell."

"I can understand that."

Vincent peered over Sam's shoulder at the bags in the corner of the room. "You ain't brought much, huh?"

"Well, in those bags are mostly clothes and stuff. Like I said, I gave everything I had away. It wasn't much really. I just figured I didn't need things like a television living out here, anyway."

"You got enough to entertain you for a long time, I can promise you."

"I'll stay here if that's alright, just until I figure out how to get a place of my own."

"Don't be worrying about that. You can stay here as long as you like. I could use a deckhand again, anyway."

"You're going to put me to work first thing tomorrow, I suspect."

"Of course. We'll start you off slow, though, to make it easy on you."

Sam rounded off the night opening up to Vincent about his last few days in Boston and how he left his job and stood up to Dee. He told him that leaving Boston was an easy decision to make. Sam could tell Vincent appreciated him opening up this time and talking about his life. It wasn't a conscious decision, though, just the way it transpired. It was the way the old man made him feel that enabled him to share personal thoughts so easily.

And Vincent loved to listen as much as he did to talk. The old man sat back quietly while Sam told him about his journey back to Louisiana.

"And that was it, I got on the bus and didn't look back," Sam said, finishing his spiel.

"I told you before you left this place gets in your blood."

"And you're right about that, it does. One of the things that made me want to come back down here the most was the thought of getting to know more about who my parents were. It pulled at me like nothing had ever in my entire life. I figured being here was a fresh start—a fresh start and the opportunity to feel closer to them."

Vincent stood and stuck his mug in the sink. He walked back to Sam at the table and put his hands on his shoulders. "I gotta hit the sack if we gonna be up early tomorrow. You'll have to sleep on a cot I got stashed in the closet."

"No problem," Sam said and went to the closet to grab the cot out.

Bellies full of fish made both men sluggish and soon they retired to their beds. Setting up the fold-up cot took Sam only a few moments. As he finished throwing a few blankets and a pillow on it, rumbles of thunder that were faint earlier in the evening were now loud thuds that rattled the old shack. A late-summer thunderstorm started to rage outside with howling winds and clattering thunder. It was the best sleep Sam had gotten in weeks.

Eight

As soon as the sun started to peak over the horizon, Vincent was stirring in the kitchen, stumbling around in the near dark to brew a pot of coffee. Sam, who had spent the night in the front room of the shack on a cot, woke up to the clatter of ceramic mugs clinking against each other. He had slept well through the night, despite the fact that he had seldom rested when it was dark outside for the past few years. The sound of the rain pattering on the tin roof that persisted throughout the early morning hours had comforted him.

Sam sat up on the cot, his long, blond hair sticking up in several directions, and yawned with a simultaneous stretch.

"Good morning. You slept alright?" Vincent asked.

"Yeah, I slept surprisingly well," Sam mumbled as he yawned again.

"This pot will be done soon and then we can get started. It's not too early for you, is it?" Vincent asked with a grin.

Sam, his eyes barely open, only smiled back.

"Today, we gonna go check my traps I reset last night. Might have caught some more catfish," Vincent said as he tucked a gray T-shirt into faded blue jeans.

"That sounds like a plan." Sam walked over to his duffle bag to put on some clothes. "What else do we have on the agenda for today?"

"Well, that's depending what's on the lines. If we don't catch, we'll set some more. Living off the land isn't easy to predict. So it's hard to make a plan. Some days you won't catch and you have to figure out what to do to bring in money and food. I know I told you this before, but it ain't easy. You gotta want this kind of life."

"I'm here and I'm ready," Sam said as he finished pulling a white T-shirt over his head and walking to the kitchen table.

"Good, that's the attitude to have." Vincent walked over to his stove-top, tin percolator to check the coffee. "Alright, now we in business."

Vincent poured two cups, then sat at the table with Sam. Vincent took a big gulp of the hot coffee and exhaled loudly. Sam held his mug with two hands, stuck his nose over the rim, and breathed in the aroma.

"Boy, I'm telling you, there's something about a cup of coffee in the mornings," Vincent said with a satisfied smile. He slipped on his white rubber boots, which were tucked just under the table, and he pushed his blue jeans into them. Picking up his sagging pants as he stood back upright, he went to his bedroom and came back with another pair of white boots, these much less worn than the ones he donned. He handed them to Sam. "Here, try these. Had an extra pair lying around. Hope they fit. If you gonna be a fisherman, you gotta look the part."

Sam slipped his right foot in. "Thanks. They fit perfect."

"Good. We call that some swamp Reeboks."

Sam laughed at Vincent's serious tone. "Why are they white?"

"That's a good question. It's kinda a tradition for fishermen to wear them. For me, why I like them, is because the white reflects the sun and doesn't get as hot as black boots. But who knows what kinda answers you would get if you asked a hundred different fishermen."

Sam stood up and spun around in place. "Look like a Cajun yet?" He wore a white, V-neck T-shirt and faded blue jeans tucked into his new boots. He was certain that he looked like a younger, beardless version of Vincent.

Vincent looked Sam up and down. "Almost, hold on one second." The old man disappeared into the back room and returned with a red trucker-style hat. "Here, give this a try."

Sam pushed his hair back and stuck on the cap, which sat high atop his head. He stuck out his arms and shrugged, asking for Vincent's opinion.

"Now you look the part," Vincent said with a laugh. "But we gonna make sure you can walk the walk. Come on, let's get a move on and get started."

The two walked outside with their coffee and hopped into Ole Blue. The boat was still hitched onto the truck from the night before. Vincent made the drive north to the boat landing and the two were riding in Vincent's skiff down Little Bayou Pigeon in no time, the sun just barely over the trees.

It was early enough in the morning to catch steam rising into the air, up from the water and dissipating after only a few vertical feet. Besides that, the swamp was just as Sam had remembered. This time, he didn't have a deadline to be back anywhere. What he was experiencing was going to be his life, his daily routine, and it was still an odd thought for him, something he knew would take time to get used to. He couldn't help but smile at the thought of it as he sat on the milk crate in front of Vincent's skiff with the wind blowing across his face.

Sam yelled above the cry of the motor when they reached Murphy Lake, where Vincent had set his trotlines the day before. "Wow, this lake is beautiful." The surface of the lake, a fat, round body of water not far from the Atchafalaya River, was calm and flat like a sheet of glass, reflecting thin clouds that streaked across the amber sky. Murphy Lake stretched a half-mile across the swamp, bordered by a dense tangle of cypress and black willow trees, the latter often growing so thick together that it was impossible to navigate a boat through them.

Sam turned his attention from the lake toward Vincent. He still marveled how Vincent drove the boat with such casualness. The old man sat back on his crate, squinting as he piloted his boat in the direction of the rising sun, though at times he'd stand to get a better look at the water ahead. Still, every move was relaxed and natural. When Vincent wanted to, he could push the rig up to forty-five miles per hour. But he usually kept the boat at speeds around thirty, just fast enough to get where he needed to go.

Sam looked around as the boat skidded to a halt. "Is your line nearby?"

"Almost. Let me show you a little secret. Some people, they hang fluorescent flags near their lines so they don't forget where they at. Like some fella has over there." Vincent pointed into the distance at the bright orange flagging hanging from a cypress branch. "Tell me what's wrong with that."

Sam contemplated for a second before responding. "I'm not exactly sure. That actually seems like a good idea."

"It is if you want people messing with your lines. Always use nature as a reminder where your lines are. That way, you don't get no one trying to steal your catch. And you don't leave trash all over the Basin." Vincent motored up the bank a few more yards before pointing again. "See that cypress with the hole in the middle, just up the bank there?"

"Yeah, I see it."

"That's where my line starts. Consider this lesson number one for the day." Vincent drove toward the lone cypress.

"Is that how you remember how to navigate the bayous so easily without maps?"

"Yep. Once you go down them a few times, you start to remember landmarks. All the bayous look a certain way and different trees stick in your head. Then if you been down the same bayous for the past seventy or so years, it kinda starts to become second nature."

Sam thought the task seemed impossible. Nearly every bayou and lake he'd been down looked identical. Though each was unique in beauty, they all essentially were covered with trees and were full of water. The only place he'd remembered so far had been the long canal leading to Riley Bayou. He figured it would take a while to commit the wild landscape to memory.

"Alright, let's see what we got. Go grab the end of the line and pull it up," Vincent said as they neared the lines.

When the boat floated close enough to the line, Sam reached over the side of Vincent's boat and grabbed a thick, black rope. He ran his hands down the line and toward the water. "It's heavy, Vin." He pulled up on the rope cautiously.

"That's a good sign. Don't worry. Keep pulling up."

Sam picked up on the rope and, to his surprise, the first hook had a decent-sized catfish on it. He pulled on the line some more and the adjacent hook yielded another catch.

"Not too shabby, huh?" Vincent said, patting Sam on the back. "That's some good looking catfish."

"What do you use for bait?"

"Fresh cut fish. Always fresh and never frozen."

"You sound like a fast food commercial," Sam said with a grin as he looked up at Vincent.

Vincent laughed. "That's the secret, my friend. Well, let's get these fish in the boat."

The catfish on the first hook squirmed and splashed in the water. Sam was hesitant to grab it, the memory—and the wound—still fresh from the day before. He figured if he could barely handle a dead one, how was he going to rope in a live one?

"I'm not sure I'll be able to do this, Vin." Sam held the rope so that the catfish's head stuck slightly out of the water. It started wriggling, making ripples in the water.

"Don't be afraid of it. It's just a measly ole catfish. Don't let what happened yesterday bother you. Just watch out for them barbs on the sides, too."

With Vincent's encouragement Sam slung the first fish into the boat, still attached to the line. He slowly inched his hand toward the slimy fish, placing it in the right position to avoid getting stuck. As he wrangled the hook out of its mouth it flopped around.

"There you go, boy. You did a good job. And no blood this time," Vincent said as he looked on.

"OK, that wasn't so bad." Sam placed it in a metal tub

in the front of the boat. He repeated the task six more times, bringing in a catfish and loading it in the boat. By the time he got to the last hook, he was feeling confident. He splashed his hands down into the water and grabbed the line. This end was drooping badly in the water and it was hard for Sam to lift. He used both hands to try to unveil what was on the other end of the line, lapping his fingers just below the surface of the brown water. "Vin, this one is tough. It must be a huge fish."

"Keep on pulling. It might be snagged on something."

Sam pulled until a large splash of water flew in his face, nearly knocking him off of his feet and into the lake. He was leaning over the side of the boat still when the prehistoric beast lunged out of the water, its white mouth and teeth springing toward him with the intent to kill. Sam didn't have time to think. All he knew was that he needed to get back to the safety of the middle of the boat. He forced his body backward as hard as he could, straining his muscles, pushed to the limit. He slammed his back against the opposite wall of the boat, just narrowly missing being clamped in the jaws of an alligator that was hooked on Vincent's trotline.

Sam gasped for air, his eyes wide open with a look of shock. His heart hammered in his chest. What little confidence he had displayed just moments before while sticking his hands in the water faded as he sat on the bottom of the boat in terror.

"You OK?" Vincent yelled from the back of his boat. He walked over to check on Sam, then started laughing.

"I almost got eaten by an alligator," Sam said between quick, short breaths. "What's funny about that?"

"Sorry, boy, but it was a little funny. You got your first

alligator sighting, alright. And it was a hoot." Vincent continued with a wheezing laugh, bending down and slapping his knee.

Sam stood up to glance back at the six-foot killer, floating on the top of the water, staring at the two men as if it was sizing them up. "Now what do we do?"

Vincent used a finger to wipe tears from his eyes and regain composure, but still with a smile on his face. "That hook ain't no more good. I'll have to cut it off."

Vincent casually picked up the line just inches from the gator's head and lifted it enough to cut the string attached to the main line. The gator wasn't pleased with Vincent getting so close and swung its tail around and splashed water at them. And just like that, it disappeared into the murky water.

Sam looked at Vincent with a surprised expression. "So, is fending off gators a part of your daily routine?"

"Aw, you didn't get bothered by that?" Vincent said, trying to hide a grin. "He's just a little baby, anyway."

"Yeah, well, I usually like to get past lunch before I'm on an animal's menu for the day. That was crazy. And you just cut him off the line like it was nothing."

"They ain't all that scary after you've dealt with them a while. Don't get me wrong, you gotta respect the power they got. But you learn how to handle them after a while."

Sam was still a bit shaken, but he was starting to recover. His hands still shook, but his breathing returned to normal as he sat down on his milk crate seat. "Well, see an alligator: check," he said, drawing a check in the air with his finger.

"The good news is we got a good catch this morning. The even better news is I got some money to get some more gas for the week."

"Are you not going to eat any of these?"

"I might save one for supper. But the rest I'm gonna bring to the buyer and sell. Prices are good for a pound right now. Ole Vin's been running low on funds so we can't eat everything we catch. Some days we gonna have to catch for other people. We'll re-bait the line and come back and check them this afternoon. Now we gotta catch some more bait. That's gonna be lesson number two."

Vincent started his boat motor. He steered the skiff a few yards down the muddy bank of the lake before killing the engine. He picked up a balled-up net from a bucket next to where he sat and stretched it out. "This is a cast net. This one takes a little while before you get the hang of it. But just watch."

Vincent used his left hand to grab the bulk of the net, which contained small weights on the bottom section. In his right hand, he held a rope attached to the net. He reared back like he was about to toss a shot put and flung the net into the water. It outstretched completely in the air before falling a few yards from the boat, the weights making a popping sound when they broke the surface of the water. The net sunk out of sight with bubbles rising to the surface of the water. Vincent used the rope he held in his right hand to pull it back to the boat. He lifted the drenched net out of the water and with it came a handful of wriggling, pocket-sized fish.

Vincent flopped the net on the floor of the boat, and water streamed toward Sam's boots. The old man bent down and picked up one of the fish and held it up with two fingers. "It's as easy as that."

Sam knelt beside the net and inspected the trapped fish.

"Seriously, though, you make this look way too easy."

Vincent shook the net, and the fish dropped onto the boat floor. Then he headed back to where his trotline was set.

Sam's hands were steady again, enough for him to take the fish and per Vincent's instructions, hook them just right to entice more catfish.

"You ready?" Vincent asked as the last hook was baited.

"Where are we headed, back to the boat landing?" Sam leaned over the side of the boat and rinsed his hands off in the lake. He made sure the alligator wasn't lurking nearby.

Vincent sat down on the milk crate seat. "Yep."

"Do we have enough time to swing by Riley Bayou?"

Vincent lit one of his hand-rolled cigarettes and smiled. "I figured you'd want to head that way." He exhaled a mouthful of smoke. "Of course we have some time."

Vincent and Sam reached Riley Bayou after cruising through the swamp for twenty minutes. The bayou was dimly lit, as the sun was partially blocked by a sheet of clouds. Down the bayou, Sam spotted an alligator lazily making its way across to the other side.

"And this one couldn't have been my first gator sighting?" Sam pointed to the creature.

Vincent stood up to get a peek. "Hey, at least you'll never forget the first time you seen a gator."

"You're right about that." Sam perked up as the houseboat came into view. The old structure was still sagging in the water just like it had been when they left it last. Finally, he thought, he'd get to return to the houseboat. The aged home hadn't left his thoughts since he first laid eyes on it.

"Go grab that post, will you?" Vincent instructed. He

parked the boat parallel to the porch so Sam could secure the vessel to one of the posts of the houseboat with a rope.

When Sam did, they both got out of the skiff.

"You want to look around like we did last time?" Vincent asked.

"I kind of just want to sit here for a while, if that's OK?" Sam looked around the porch. "I've been waiting to get back here since the moment we left."

"Sure, we can do that."

Vincent leaned back against one of the posts, fumbling with a pack of tobacco to roll a cigarette, while Sam sat cross-legged near the doorway of the porch. He felt back at home, as if his parents were nearby. It was the same feeling he had when he first visited Riley Bayou. He was at ease, warm, and comfortable, feeling like he never wanted to leave the area. Again, the thought crossed his mind that Vincent certainly was right: being in Louisiana—in Riley Bayou, especially— was where he belonged.

In that moment, he thought of a way to spend his time in Louisiana. A perfect way to keep the connection to his parents always strong. "Do you think this old thing could be fixed up? I mean, instead of moving everything from here and to your house, what if we fixed it up and used it?"

Vincent looked toward Sam, a bit of surprise on his face. "This thing needs a lot of work, boy. A lot of work."

"But do you think it could be done? Getting it to float properly again and all."

Vincent looked around the houseboat, assessed the damage, and attempted to calculate what would need to be fixed. "Yeah, it can definitely be done, but that's gonna take some money and a good bit of time."

"Well I don't have much money, but I've got plenty of time and I'm willing to learn."

Vincent raised his eyebrows and shook his head. "Boy, boy," he said, almost reluctantly. "I'm not making any promises. But we can go pass by Chris' house on the way back from selling the fish and see if he has some spare wood we can use. I know he had some foam he was thinking about using for a houseboat one day. It'll take some convincing, but he may let us use them."

Sam stood up with excitement. "Really? You think we could?"

Vincent laughed. "As long as you do the heavy lifting. If you lucky, we might even be able to get Chris to help us out."

"Would we have to pay him?"

"Maybe a little bit, but that's not what he's worried about. Around here, you work for someone and you repay the favor by working for them. You see what I mean?"

"Absolutely, I'm game for that. Almost like the whole bartering thing. This way you're bartering your work—I get it."

"Chris is better than me at that stuff. He builds houses around Bayou Pigeon and has built camps here and there."

Sam rubbed the outside of the houseboat. The yellow paint cracked and chipped with the slightest touch, revealing the grey boards beneath. As his hand continued to rest on the houseboat, the gears in his head turned more. "So, if it's possible to fix this place and get it safe to stand on, what about living on it?"

Vincent tilted his head to the side, his eyebrows rose, and his forehead wrinkled. "You want to live in the Basin?"

"Well, maybe. After I learn everything, and can do what

you do on my own. I mean, I'll be needing a place to call my own eventually."

"Sam, if you got the desire, I believe you can do it." Vincent's tone seemed uncertain, and the old man was cautious when he spoke. "But, trust me, it'll take a little while before we can get this thing in working order. It ain't gonna be easy."

Sam sensed the old man's hesitance. He couldn't blame him, though. Sam knew he had a lot to learn. He wanted to convince Vincent anyway. "I figured it wouldn't be. But what a better way to get acquainted with the place I was born than to live in it? I'm sure getting this place fixed back up would make them both happy."

"Sam, just knowing you were here right now and healthy would've made them happy."

"Well, do you think I'd be able to do it?"

"I ain't one to stop anyone from living how they see fit. If you want to live out here, I don't see why you can't."

"Then it's a plan." Sam paced around the porch, looking from one place to another to get a better grasp of what had to be done. He hadn't even thought about living on the old houseboat before, but hearing Vincent say it could be fixed was all he needed to ignite the spark within him.

"You ever do any construction or any house remodeling?"

"Well, no." Sam turned back to walk toward Vincent.

"Any painting or working with your hands?"

"Here and there, I guess."

Vincent laughed and shook his head.

"I'm a fast learner, Vin," Sam said to make his case. "And I'm a hard worker."

"If you anything like your daddy, I believe you. But you got a good teacher. I'll show you everything you need to know. So, if we going visit with Chris, we better head on out before he leaves. No telling where he'll be come lunch time. And we still gotta sell these fish."

"Yeah, that's right. I almost forgot about the catfish. How long will they stay fresh in the heat like this?"

"Out in the sun, hardly long at all."

Vincent boarded the skiff. He opened a storage compartment in the bow and pulled out a large burlap sheet. "But all you gotta do is wet this thing." He dipped the burlap into the bayou. "Then stick it on top the fish. They'll be good for a few more hours now."

Sam walked over toward the boat to get a better look. "I feel like I should have a pen and paper taking notes."

"You'd need a pretty big notebook. Come on, let's get a move on."

They were soon back out of the Atchafalaya and arrived at a blue metal building bearing the bright, ruby letters 'Cajun Seafood' on a sign near its roof. Sam exited Ole Blue and grabbed the tub topped to the rim with catfish from the floor of the skiff. He then followed Vincent toward the building. Two men stood near an outside freezer door talking; they nodded at Sam as he set down the tub of fish, and he Vincent walked by.

Vincent entered a nearby office with Sam close behind. A man was sitting at a desk talking on the phone. When he saw Sam and Vincent enter, he smiled, held up his hand for the men to come in, and whispered he'd be off in a second.

"This is your other lesson for the day: making some money," Vincent mouthed lightly to Sam.

Joe, the owner of Cajun Seafood, looked a lot like the other fishermen hanging around the outside of the joint: tan, rugged, and donning a ratty shirt accompanied by blue jeans. Of course, he was sporting the white rubber boots that Vincent had explained were a part of Cajun culture.

"Vin, what you got for me today?" Joe said as he hung up the phone.

"We didn't do too bad. Got a little mess of catfish. And by the way, this is Sam. Sam, this is Joe."

"Nice to meet you," Joe said, getting up from his chair and shaking Sam's hand. "You following around this ole man?"

"Trying to, but he moves fast," Sam said.

"How much channel cats going for a pound right now?" Vincent asked Joe. "The price still good?"

"I can give you $3."

"We'll take that," Vincent said with a smile over to Sam. "This man here got the fairest prices you gonna find."

"What, you showing him around the bayou or something?" Joe asked.

"Sam just moved down here from Boston. He's gonna be staying with me a while."

"No kidding. Well, welcome to Louisiana. How long you staying?" Joe asked, crossing his arms.

"Hopefully for good. Or at least until Vin kicks me out."

"Or until you kick him out, huh?" Joe laughed and patted Vincent on the back. "Let's go get y'all rung up."

The three men walked out of Joe's office to a stainless steel table with a scale hanging near it, just in front of a freezer door.

"Plop them on the scale one by one," Vincent said.

Sam placed the biggest one first: 6 pounds. He placed the second: just under 5 pounds. He continued until the last one was weighed. Each time he laid a fish on the scale, Joe jotted down the figure. After the last, Joe tallied the numbers. "OK. Y'all had close to 25 pounds of fish. At $3 a pound, that's $75. I'll go inside and get y'all some cash. I'll be right back, fellas."

"Man, that's good for just an hour of work," Sam said to Vincent.

"Yeah, we didn't do too bad. That'll be good enough for the whole week, maybe more."

"You're going to have to quit making it look so easy. I'm going to think I can live off the land sooner than I should."

"It ain't always this smooth. I wish it was."

Joe walked back to the men with the money and handed it to Vincent. "Thank y'all. Have a good one. And Sam, good luck out here. If you need anything, give me a call. Watch out for this one here and make sure he don't get you into any trouble." Joe smiled and pointed to Vincent, before walking over to another fisherman that had pulled up with a morning catch.

Sam and Vincent waved before they hopped back into Vincent's old Ford.

Sam scooted onto the blue bench seat and snapped on his seat belt. "That was easy."

"Yep. That's another thing, we need to make you legal."

"What do you mean?"

"You gonna need a commercial fishing license. We can't have you fishing out here without a license. Wildlife and fisheries catches you helping me without a license and they gonna give you a ticket."

"Got it. Another thing to add to the list."

"We'll head to Chris' and see if he's home first."

Vincent drove back toward the Atchafalaya levee and the road that paralleled it. Sam thought of the moment he first gazed upon the earthen wall, wondering what it protected and what lay on the other side. He had initially thought it appeared a bit ominous, as he looked at it without knowing what it was. But now, he envisioned the levees as the gates to the wilderness—a place he saw as his future home.

Vincent pulled up to Chris' house, a trailer not far from the boat landing, that was positioned directly across from the levee. Chris' mobile home was newer than those around him. His didn't yet have the distinct green growth of the others in the area. Like most all his neighbors, Chris had not one but multiple boats lining his front yard.

"OK, well it looks like he's home. Come on," Vincent said, spotting Chris' truck.

Sam followed Vincent down the gravel driveway and to Chris' doublewide. Vincent knocked on the glass window of the door and a moment later Chris opened it. Sam thought Chris looked different, probably due to the daytime lighting—and him being sober. He was alert, had a bit more color to his face, and his short hair was neatly styled. Sam thought it was also nice to see him wearing clothes.

"Uh oh, what I did?" Chris asked sarcastically.

"It's not what you did, but if you can do something?" Vincent quipped.

"I knew you were here for something." He exited his house and joined Sam and Vincent on the front porch.

"We gonna need some help," Vincent said.

"With what?"

"We fixing up that ole houseboat on Riley Bayou and we need some foam and wood. You think you can help us out?"

"Vin, you know I been saving that to build my own houseboat."

"Boy, you been saying that for years. We'll all be dead before you start building that thing. And plus, I got something more valuable than money."

"I'm listening," Chris said with his hand cupped to his ear.

Vincent pointed to Sam. "I've got a young man with plenty of energy and willing to help you work."

"Who's that?" Chris said with a raised eyebrow.

"Aw, were you so drunk that night you don't even remember seeing him come in the camp?"

Chris scratched his head and winced like he was trying to remember. "Um, no, I don't think so."

"Good god, boy. Well, this is Sam Miller. He just moved here. He's my family and he's gonna be staying down here."

Sam smiled after hearing Vincent call him family.

"Nice to meet you," Chris said as he shook Sam's hand.

Sam nodded. "Nice to meet you, too. Again."

"OK, and what's the catch after all this help?" Chris asked Vincent, getting back to business.

"No catch. And if you help us out with fixing it up a bit, I'll throw in that ole Johnson outboard motor I've been working on that you been begging me to have."

Chris rubbed his chin for a second, thinking over the deal. Then he smiled and outstretched his hand. "You got a deal, buddy. I been after you to sell me that thing for years and now you gonna give it away. There ain't no way I'm passing that deal up."

Chris and Vincent shook hands, then Chris grabbed a hold of Sam's and shook it.

"I got plenty of projects I could use your help on," Chris said to him.

Vincent shook his finger at Chris. "Not so fast. There's plenty of work to be done on that houseboat."

"What y'all doing with that thing, anyway?" Chris asked.

Vincent motioned to Sam. "It was for his parents."

"No kidding. Well, that's pretty cool. I've been to that thing once a few years ago and it was in bad shape then. I guess we have our work cut out for us."

"We sure do. But, Sam here wants to make it his home. So, we'll try to go as fast as we can," Vincent said.

"Really? Well, when y'all want to start? I ain't got another house scheduled to build until November, so I'm free for the next two months."

"How about first thing next week?" Sam asked.

"Sure," Chris agreed. "Look, y'all come out to the backyard and we'll see what y'all might want to use."

The three men walked to the rear of the trailer into a backyard full of piles of wood, metal, and other scraps. Chris even had another two boats sitting back there among the piles.

"Here's that foam." Chris pointed out large rectangular blocks of white foam to use for flotation under the houseboat. "I been saving this for years. You lucky I owe you."

Vincent pointed to a pile of gray boards. "And that ole cypress, we'll use that, too."

Chris raised his hands in the air. "The cypress, too?

That's some good wood right there. I don't know if I can part with that."

"Well fine. I guess that ole Johnson motor will keep sitting in my backyard," Vincent said.

Chris sighed loudly. "Alright, alright. Just leave me some leftover, OK?"

Sam thought it strange to hear the men discuss materials without once ever bringing up an exchange of money. Being accustomed to always having a price for something, he thought the bartering practice was much more practical. Maybe what Chris and Vincent had stashed in their backyards was collateral rather than piles of junk. He thought perhaps that's why so many people had multiple boats in the area; maybe they were bartering tools.

After Vincent and Chris discussed the materials they'd need, including a few items they'd have to purchase at the hardware store, Vincent clapped Chris on the back and said, "Alright, well, we heading back to the Basin. We got some more traps to check and this young man got a lot to learn. We'll see you later."

"Later," Sam said. "And thanks again for the help."

"No problem. If this old man cares enough about you to do this, I figure it must be worth it."

"He's family," Vincent said as he looked back at Chris from the driveway, "and you know how we take care of family down here."

Vincent's second reference to him as family made Sam smile again as they walked back to the truck. Not only was Vincent making him feel like he indeed had family, but it felt good to hear him say it. His first day in Louisiana was turning out to be better than he anticipated.

Nine

Vincent and Sam sat in the skiff next to the houseboat, looking over the crude images Sam had drawn that showed not just what he wanted to do with the home, but with the entire area. The early start enabled the men to take advantage of the cool September morning while they could. It was one of those rare days during the early part of the month when the humidity dropped along with the temperature, which was only in the upper 60s. But the air had a subtle crispness to it that reminded Sam of Boston during the early fall.

"Thanks for helping me recreate what it looked like when Mom and Dad lived here," Sam said. "I think this is going to turn out really great when it's all done."

Vincent whistled. "I agree, but, boy, that was a job for Vin's ole brain to try to remember."

Sam had pressed the old man for details as minute as where certain items like dishes went in the cabinets. His bundle of drawings also contained schematics for where his garden would be when he planted in the spring. He had a spot picked out for his work area, where he'd be building pirogues once he learned the trade from Vincent. Chickens seemed like a good idea, too, and he had started designing a raised coop to keep the critters high and dry whenever the land around Riley Bayou flooded. He had sketched out a new roof, full of solar panels to give him the energy he would need to power lights and other small household items. And Vincent helped him draw up a design for a rain collection system that would float next to the houseboat on a mini barge that could collect five hundred gallons of water so Sam would be able to get fresh, clean water for drinking, bathing, and cooking.

"I'm proud of you, boy. This is quite the plan you've got."

Sam beamed. He had never gotten the chance to use his mind in such a creative way before. His job back in Boston didn't require much brain power. Reading was the only way he had ever really been able to use his imagination. So the prospect of rebuilding the home was starting to feel like more than just a construction project to him. It was an outlet to express his creativity. And in a way, he saw the old houseboat like his life, tattered and in disarray, something that needed fixing but didn't have someone or something to help it along the way. Now he'd be able to breathe new life into the old home, like living in Louisiana—and spending time with Vincent—was doing to him. It was a perfect match, he thought; he and the houseboat needed a fresh start.

Chris zoomed up in a homemade skiff, similar in design and construct to Vincent's, a few minutes behind schedule. Over a cup of coffee and after a friendly scolding from Vincent, Chris joined them as they discussed their plans for getting the foam blocks up and under the houseboat. The blocks were dense and floated, so just the task of sticking them underwater was going to be difficult. Chris had a concept of tying heavy items together with a chain and draping them over the top of the foam. He presumed this would force the blocks to sink down into the water so they could slide them into place. After bolting the pieces of foam to the houseboat frame, the idea was that they could release the weights. They didn't exactly know if it would work, but that was what they were going to try.

"This plan is Cajun ingenuity at its finest," Vincent said with a proud gleam in his eye after all of the details were hashed out.

Even though he'd only known the two of them briefly, Sam quickly realized that Cajuns had an innate sense of self-reliance. For a group of people to thrive in such a wild place, he thought they definitely needed a strong will. If something couldn't be fixed, Vincent said Cajuns didn't complain about it, but found a way. It was a quality bred into the culture, something Sam was anxious to display.

"OK, so, Sam, you and Chris can go ahead and get in the water and start with them blocks," Vincent said to kick off the morning work. Vincent's part in the plan was to stand in the boat and hand over the blocks, while disposing of the old, rusted barrels that served as the original flotation.

Sam and Chris flung off their swamp Reeboks and got into their underwear while they stood in Vincent's skiff near the rear of the houseboat.

Chris jumped into the water, bobbed back up and swam on his back in the bayou.

"At least this isn't the first time I've seen you in your underwear," Sam joked to Chris. Sam and Vincent laughed while Chris looked bewildered.

"Huh?" Chris said as he swam toward the houseboat.

Sam slowly dipped his body in the bayou, hanging on to the side of Vincent's boat. "First night I was here and we came into your camp, you were passed out on the couch in nothing but your underwear."

Chris burst into laughter, as if it wasn't the first time he'd drank so much he had forgotten meeting someone. "Hey, cut me a break." He casually waded under the houseboat.

Sam cautiously followed Chris as close as he could. He was a bit hesitant about the idea of being in the water. His bare feet sunk into the thick mud underfoot. It was soft and squishy, a perfect hiding place for a gator, he thought. His mind kept replaying the alligator incident from a few days ago. But he didn't let it show that he was uneasy. He was going to work hard no matter what he was tasked with. Plus, Vincent was on gator duty, scanning the bayou now and then to ensure none of the beasts were making their way toward the houseboat. Sam felt comfortable with the old man watching his back—and apparently so did Chris.

The first step was removing the old barrels that were fixed to the under part of the houseboat. The 55-gallon metal drums were once painted a shiny black and worked as a stable base for the home. They lasted about forty years but they probably would have barely lasted another few until they were completely rusted and on the bottom of the bayou. Chris and Sam waded in the murky water up to their necks to get close enough to the bolts.

They were rusted so badly some of them needed to be snapped off with a stout plier, Chris determined.

The bolts on the first barrel, four in total, did need to be snapped off. After the remains of the barrel were removed, they used cinder blocks connected to a chain and draped it over the top of the first piece of foam to help weigh it down in the water. Only then could they position it under the houseboat. Chris' idea wasn't guaranteed to work. He had only fastened together the makeshift tools the day before. But any doubts they had about the plan were quickly put to rest when the first three-foot-high block sunk under water without error. The extra weight of the two men pulling down on the chain helped. The block went right into place and they were able to bolt it onto the frame using stainless steel strips.

Vincent watched Sam and Chris, whose heads were barely visible from under the houseboat. "Not too shabby. Looks like that fits pretty good, boys."

"I told y'all it would work," Chris boasted.

Little by little, the houseboat started to straighten out after each trip to unbolt a barrel and attach a block of foam. The badly sagging section raised up each time Sam and Chris added another small piece.

Sam had gotten comfortable with the routine, and being in the water wasn't bothering him as much anymore. He was diving underwater without hesitation, submerging his whole body and swimming under the houseboat frame, getting as close as he could to unbolt the barrels.

Instead of letting Chris take the lead on the next barrel, Sam swam up to prepare to unbolt it. He grabbed the rusty bolt with the plyer and turned it. It snapped off with ease. As he went on to the next one, he froze. In his haste to show Chris and Vincent he was a hard worker, he'd neglected to check the barrel for any creatures lurking in the shadows.

"Chris...Chris!" he shouted.

Chris swam over behind Sam. "What's up? You alright?"

"What do I do if there's a snake staring me in the face? I shouldn't make a sudden movement, right?"

A dark brown snake sat curled on top of the barrel just above the surface of the water, eye level with Sam. Its tense position meant it was ready to strike. Sam struggled to tread water light enough to keep his movements to a minimum while trying to keep his nerves from taking over. However, he felt trapped under the dark houseboat and started to feel as if he'd panic at any second.

"What's it look like?" Chris asked.

"Like a brown or black color, big head, and it's curled up and staring at me."

"Damn," Chris mumbled lightly. "Look, back out as slow as you possibly can, and right, don't make any sudden movements."

"What's going on," Vincent asked from his boat a few yards away.

"I'm pretty sure Sam found him a moccasin. I got it, though. He's coming out."

Sam slowly backed up from the barrel. As he did, the snake started to move, alarmed by the motion, but Sam was able to escape unscathed.

Chris swam under the house and disappeared. He came out with the snake curled around his right hand and tattooed arm. "It was a moccasin alright. Pretty nice size, too. About three feet long."

Sam hung on the side of Vincent's skiff to give his muscles a rest and to calm his breathing. "Those are venomous, aren't they?"

"Sure are," Chris said, the snake raised above his head as he swam.

Vincent shook his head. "You show off. Go throw that thing outta here, boy."

Chris laughed and swam over to the bank to let the snake go.

Again, Sam's confidence had been rattled by a swamp creature, another animal that he figured could've very well killed him just days into his new life in Louisiana. He started to question if he had what it took to survive out in the Atchafalaya.

"You did good, Sam," Vincent said, looking down at him from the skiff. "You kept your cool."

The praise from Vincent made Sam feel a bit better. Yeah, he thought, that situation was handled well. After all, he didn't get bitten and didn't panic. He figured he was already making progress.

It was nearly dark when they removed the last barrel and secured the final new piece of foam. The cool temperatures of the morning had quickly faded throughout the day, and the heat persisted well into the evening. The brisk air from sunrise was only a tease of the consistently cooler weather that was still months away. Just a half hour before sunset and the temperatures hovered around ninety degrees.

They had made three trips back to the boat landing throughout the day and the only rest they had was a few minutes to eat lunch. The three men were exhausted, but their hard work had paid off. They successfully raised the back end of the houseboat, and it sat in the water perfectly level. They'd still have to replace the rest of the old barrels on the other end because it wouldn't be long until they started to sink. They were all rusted badly on the outside, and while they hadn't developed any holes yet, Vincent suspected it was only a matter of time. But that was to be a project for another day.

Sam was sprawled on the floor of Vincent's boat, his muscles weak from the hours of swimming and treading water. He tilted his head up and looked at the houseboat. "I'd say that looks pretty good." He was proud of the work he'd done, plus his eagerness, and the situation with the water moccasin, had impressed both Vincent and Chris.

"I'd have to agree," Vincent said, sitting back on his seat in the skiff while he smoked a cigarette. "Seems like it won't be as bad as I first thought to fix this ole thing up. None of them structural supports are cracked, so it might be less work than I feared."

Chris chimed in, "Yeah, Sam, for a city boy, you ain't half bad. You work your butt off. I'm gonna be able to put you to good use in the next couple of months."

"I definitely owe you after today," Sam replied.

Chris sat in his boat parallel to Vincent's with his feet propped up. "Well, what's next?"

"I figure we'll start on the roof this week," Sam said. "Then after that, I'll start on the inside of the house, fixing boards, replacing windows and everything. Then after that it'll be small stuff like painting and touch ups."

Vincent shook his head in approval. "If you keep up at this pace, you'll be done in a month or so. I'm proud of you. Your parents would be, too."

"I'd like to think so."

"Look, I know y'all tired, but I got a proposal," Vincent said with smoke rising out from his mouth. "Sam ain't never eaten frog legs and he certainly ain't ever been frogging. I say we take him down the bayou and show him how it's done."

Chris slapped his hands together in enthusiasm and agreed. "Hell yeah, I'm game for that. As long as you driving, Vin."

"Sure, we can start in the lake by your camp. How's that sound, Sam?"

"I'm not exactly sure what frogging is, but it sounds great"

"It's practically a rite of passage here," Vincent said.

"Yep. We gonna catch bull frogs with our bare hands to eat," Chris explained.

Sam laughed. "Is there anything you Cajuns won't eat?"

"If it's got a pulse it's on the menu," Vincent said.

"Vin's fried frog legs might be the best I've ever eaten. Boy, if my momma would hear me say that she'd whoop me good, but it's true," Chris said.

"Can we consider this another one of your lessons then, Vin?" Sam asked.

Chris sat upright on the seat in his boat. "You gonna have a whole lot of lessons tonight. Alright, well I'm headed to the camp. I'm gonna change into some dry clothes and grab a bite to eat. Y'all meet me over there." Chris started the motor to his skiff and waved before taking off down the bayou, leaving Sam and Vincent behind as darkness began to envelop the area.

The water settled quickly in the bayou, and the clatter of the motor grew fainter by the second. The noises of the Atchafalaya were again audible as Sam and Vincent rested in the skiff.

"You really are a hard worker," Vincent said, interrupting the clatter of birds and buzzing insects.

Sam sat up, his blue underwear still soaked, and ran his hands through his damp hair. "Thanks. Guess I've been working for so long it's kind of second nature these days."

"You a Cajun, there's no doubt about that."

"Really, you think so?"

"Absolutely. Being Cajun ain't about where you live so much as it is the kind of person you are." Vincent took a long drag on his cigarette. "And you got everything that makes a good Cajun."

Sam smiled and leaned back against his milk crate seat, squinting in the waning sunlight to inspect the work they had accomplished during the day. He exhaled and folded his hands behind his head. "It really does look good. I'm so proud of it already. I can't wait to get it looking nice."

"So what got into you, after all, wanting to rebuild the ole houseboat? It took me a little by surprise that you wanted to do something like this."

"I'm not exactly sure, really. Every time I've been in there it's been hard to leave. I feel connected to both of them when I'm in there. Then I started thinking about it fading into the swamp one day. If that happens, all those memories they made here will fade away, too. And I can't let that happen."

Vincent nodded, smashed the butt of his cigarette against the side of the boat, and lit another one. "I'm glad you came here, Sam." He puffed from his cigarette to get it lit properly. "I know what you mean. The truth is it started to become a struggle for me to look after the ole place. And if you never would've came along, I don't think I would've ever been able to get all their stuff out on my own. It woulda just sunk one day. At first I was a little hesitant about the project being too big of an undertaking, but I'm glad we doing it. It's something that needed to be done a long time ago."

"I understand it was hard for you to care for it over the years. I mean, especially with you fishing every day alone, I'm sure it was hard to keep track of everything. Let's just both be glad I found you when I did, before another flood came through and wiped the poor, old thing out for good."

"Sam, I'm glad you came along when you did. For more reasons than one."

Ten

Sam pushed the bow of Vincent's skiff away from the houseboat's porch, giving the old Cajun a clear path to drive. Vincent donned a hardhat with a Q-beam mounted to its front, similar to a miner's helmet from coal country. It was connected to a car battery in the front of the skiff via an orange extension cord. The bright light illuminated a wide, long swath of the dark swamp in a yellow hue for almost a hundred yards.

"Oh, and I made you something," Vincent said. He slowed down and fumbled around near the rear of his boat. He handed Sam a hardhat light similar to his own. It had a shiny white exterior with a black funnel surrounding a light on the front.

Sam turned the hat around and saw *'famille, amour, une vie,'* his mother's maxim, inscribed in black words. It was complemented by a small, crude drawing of a fleur-de-lis.

"Vin, this is awesome. Thanks a lot. I love it."

"You're welcome. I made it yesterday while you were working on the houseboat plans. I figured we'd be able to cap off a hard day's work with a fun night."

Sam looked up at him and smiled. He stuck the hardhat

atop his head and attached the extension cord's clips to another car battery Vincent had stored in the bow of the skiff. Sam's light came to life. "Hey, it works pretty good."

"Now, don't be thinking I made it as good as mine. I couldn't make it bright like mine so you seeing more frogs than me. We get a little competitive out here sometimes."

"I'm still a little hazy on the details of this whole frogging thing."

"I'm gonna show you in a second. Just wait 'til we out the bayou and in that big canal."

As Vincent made the turn into the canal outside of Riley Bayou, the yellow light penetrated deep into the swamp. The heat had yet to fade, and the humidity was as oppressive as ever. The temperatures meant the creatures of the Atchafalaya were out in full force, buzzing about loudly.

Sam flipped off his light, and looked up to see thousands of stars twinkling in the sky, the only light, aside from Vincent's, in an otherwise black landscape. The swamp was the darkest place he'd ever been, and he had never laid his eyes on so many stars before. The pitch darkness seemed like it could be a scary place to be at night, despite the beauty he witnessed during the day. Vincent said Cajuns had long told stories of a werewolf-like creature lurking in the shadows of the swamp called the Rougarou, and it was easy for Sam to see why. Snakes, alligators, an array of bugs, wild hogs, and even black bears roamed the landscape at night. As Vincent's light beamed all over the green jumble of trees, Sam thought viewing the Atchafalaya from the safety of a boat was probably a better way to enjoy its beauty at night.

"Now, there's a few things you need to know," Vincent said as bugs, attracted by the light, swarmed around his head.

"We'll practice before we get to Chris' camp. Turn your light back on so you scan the right side of the bank. I'll look on the left. What you looking for is white, yellowish eyes, and sometimes you'll even see a white belly. Sometimes, you may only see one eye. And it's important to note two things: something reflecting too bright is probably trash and red eyes is alligators."

"Right. I'll definitely make note of the last."

"When we see one big enough, I'll slowly bring you to him and you stretch out your hands over the front of the boat. Right before you about to touch him, snatch with both hands and don't let go. Got it?"

"Sounds easy enough."

"And don't grab a snake."

"Definitely got that one."

"Alright, let's go."

Vincent sped off down the canal into the darkness, peering toward the left bank for bullfrogs among the tangle of bushes and cypress tree roots that rise out of the ground called knees. Sam scanned to the right of the boat as he was instructed. He was a bit unsure of exactly how he'd spot a frog out of all the trees. Sure, the light was indeed bright. But he thought spotting an eye smaller than a dime on a bank full of debris, sticks, and bushes was easier said than done.

"Here we go. We got a big ole one right here," Vincent exclaimed as he slowed the boat and turned it portside. He had spotted the first frog of the night. It was resting on a log jetting out from the canal's bank.

"Where?" Sam asked as he stood, trying to pick out an eye or some other feature.

Vincent gestured toward the bank. "Look to where my

light is pointed. He's on the log facing us and he's a big one."

Sam positioned his light to where Vincent's was and squinted. "Wait, yeah. I'm pretty sure I see him."

"OK, good. Now, I'm gonna creep up real slow and put you directly in front of him."

Sam got into position in the front of the boat. He laid out across the bow and let his arms dangle over the water.

"Keep your light on him. Don't take it off or he'll jump," Vincent instructed.

Sam stayed motionless as he got closer to the frog, until he could see every detail of the amphibian. Its white belly faced him, bounded by a green body with brown spots. Vincent was right—it was huge. It sat still, perched on the floating log. Sam expected it to hop off at any second, but the behemoth seemed unaware of him approaching.

"OK, we almost there," Vincent said.

Sam slowly moved his hands into position as the boat inched near the log, his stomach lying flat on the boat's bow, his upper half suspended above the water. When his hands were only a few inches from the frog's face, he lunged forward with both hands, so much so he almost flew out of the skiff into the water. He felt the squishy body of the amphibian wriggle about in his hands, so slippery it almost slid right out. He held on and pulled back, trying to slow his motion. "I got it!" He raised up from the bow holding the giant as tight as he could above his head. It kicked in his hands, the legs going just as fast as Sam's heart. "Man, that was a rush of adrenaline right there."

"Good job, boy. I half expected you'd let him drop back in the water."

"Well I'm glad to see you have confidence in me."

Vincent laughed. "Here, stick him in this cage so we can keep him alive and fresh." He grabbed a wire, rectangular cage from the storage compartment in the bow of the skiff. Like much of Vincent's belongings, it appeared decades old. Sam shoved the frog into the cage.

"Alright, we'll continue on the way and see if we can spot anymore."

Sam wiped the slime and mud from the frog on his pants and sat back on the milk crate, quickly peering back to the canal bank to spot his next target as Vincent sped off.

"Hey, I think I see one," Sam yelled out above the noise of the outboard motor. He pointed to a spot on an exposed bank, and Vincent slowed the boat.

"Nope, that's a piece of trash. Keep on looking. It'll come to you."

Along the way to Grand Lake, Vincent pointed out a few more frogs, though he didn't stop again. The main bayous and waterways of the Atchafalaya they traveled on weren't home to as many frogs as the more secluded areas of the swamp. None of the specimens they saw were large enough to keep, so they continued motoring on.

Sam and Vincent pulled up to find Chris smoking a cigarette and drinking a beer, waiting for them on the pier in Grand Lake.

"It's about time y'all showed up," Chris said as he hopped into the boat and pushed it away from the pier so Vincent could turn around.

"I had to break him in a little bit. Look, he caught his first one." Vincent shined his light into the cage that held the lone frog.

"Alright, nice job, buddy, I'll let you grab first, then.

We'll take turns. If you miss, it's my turn. Then if I miss, it's yours again."

Sam scooted the milk crate farther toward the front of the boat to make room for Chris. "Vin told me it gets competitive between the two of you. I have a feeling you'll be grabbing frogs all night with rules like that."

"Don't let him get in your head with all that, Sam," Vincent said. "He ain't as good as he thinks he is. But I can promise you he will get competitive."

Vincent drove down one of the many bodies of water that poured into Grand Lake. The one he chose was small and shallow, but had plenty of places for a frog to hide. The Atchafalaya, with its warm, fresh water and vegetation, perfect for hiding, laying eggs, and finding a mate, was heaven for a bullfrog. Picking any corner of the expansive swamp yielded at least a few. Vincent relayed that the key was finding an area that hadn't been picked over by other frog hunters as well as having a keen set of eyes.

Vincent drove slowly through the slough, carefully scanning the base of cypress trees and every spot he thought a frog might hide.

Sam, too, kept his eyes peeled as best he could.

"Alright, this time I think I've really got one," Sam said, pointing into the darkness.

"Nice spot," Vincent said after looking over to confirm it. He motored slowly toward the frog, and both he and Sam fixed their lights directly on the critter as Chris sat in between them and watched.

Sam moved into position. He drifted toward the frog with his hands outstretched. When he was inches from its face he lunged forward. "He got away," he shouted.

"Aw, come on now. You can't be missing like that," Vincent said, reversing the boat back into the middle of the slough. "You miss like that and we ain't gonna have enough to eat."

Chris snatched the hardhat from Sam. "And more importantly, now it's time for me to grab." He sat in the front of the boat on the crate seat.

"Don't get too comfortable up there. I'll be back," Sam said as he pointed at Chris.

It didn't take long before Vincent spotted another frog, which sent Chris into position in the front of the skiff. The creature was bigger than the first one Sam had grabbed.

"This thing here is huge, boy," Vincent claimed, putting pressure on Chris. "If you miss this one, you ain't never stepping foot in my boat again. You better not miss."

"Can it, old man," Chris yelled back as he lay out across the bow. He lunged forward at the creature, which sent water splashing in several directions.

"You get him?" Vincent asked.

Chris grumbled as he slapped at the water in frustration. He came back into the boat with nothing but wet hands.

Vincent couldn't contain his laughter and Sam chimed in, too. Chris grinned and shook his head before joining them. Chris ceded the hardhat light back to Sam. "Alright, go ahead and laugh."

Sam grabbed his light and stuck it back on his head. "You know if I catch more than you tonight, you'll have gotten beaten by a city boy from Boston."

"There's plenty of night ahead of us. I'll take my chances. Just wait until the next one," Chris quipped.

Vincent spotted another frog not long after the words

left Chris' mouth. Sam got back up in front of the boat and the routine continued. This frog was perched on a log, and Sam spotted him right away. He caught it and the next four after that, but missed on the sixth attempt, and then Chris caught a few. The men continued to catch, miss, then catch some more. For four hours they scoured lakes, bayous and canals for glowing eyes of a frog under their powerful head-lamps. All in all, they roped in thirty-four frogs, a good night's catch and plenty enough for supper.

"So, I think the official count is Sam twenty-one, Chris thirteen," Vincent said as he slowly drove back out into Grand Lake from a small bayou. "Chris, I hate to say it, but Sam whooped you good."

"Yeah, yeah, yeah, y'all laugh it up. I took it easy on you, Sam. Just wait until next time," Chris said.

Sam shrugged and patted Chris on the shoulder. "Next time Vin's not letting you back in his boat, remember? I'll be the one grabbing them all."

"Y'all just leave some for me to eat."

Vincent shot off into the lake and shouted above the motor, "We can fry 'em up tomorrow after we get done working on the roof."

It was nearly midnight when Vincent pulled the boat back up to Chris' camp. "See you tomorrow," Sam shouted as Chris waved farewell and retired inside his camp.

"That was fun. I like Chris," Sam told Vincent as they headed back toward Riley Bayou. Sure, Chris was a little rough around the edges and he drank way too much, but Sam could tell he was a good guy.

"That's good. Chris is a good friend to have."

Before they reached their destination, Vincent motored

out to the middle of a lake not far from Riley Bayou and killed the engine.

"Why did we stop?" Sam asked as the boat skidded to a halt.

"Let's enjoy a little quiet for a bit. I like to sit out in the middle of a lake at night like this sometimes. It's a good way to relax and clear your head. Plus, clear night like it is, stars are too beautiful not to look at."

From the rear of the boat, Vincent lit a cigarette while he sat on the milk crate and leaned on the outboard motor. Sam crawled onto the floor and leaned against the front of the skiff.

Vincent opened his ice chest and cracked open a beer. He extended another can to Sam. "How about a beer?"

"No thanks, Vin."

"Man, come on. Relax a little bit. You deserve a cold one after the hard day we've had."

"Really, I'm fine."

Vincent put the beer back into his ice chest and closed it. "I'm guessing you don't drink."

"No, not really."

"Well, ain't nothing wrong with that. To each his own." Vincent said before taking a gulp.

That might've been the end of it, since Sam had remained relatively quiet about much of his upbringing throughout the conversations they had so far, and Vincent didn't pry. But, after everything Vincent shared with him, Sam thought he owed it to him to tell him about himself, and what he had been through.

He took a deep breath before speaking in a stiff, cold tone.

"After Evelyn died, Nathan started drinking. It started out slow at first, but by the time I was fourteen he was drinking heavily. He would get home at night, drunk as can be, and pass out on the sofa in our living room. I still remember the way he reeked of whiskey."

Sam closed his eyes and thought back to those miserable days. Even after all this time, the memories were easy to summon. He'd be working on his homework when Nathan would wake up and suddenly have a chore that Sam had to do right away.

"When he was awake, he always had something he wanted me to do. And he'd yell and carry on until I did it. He had this crazed obsession with keeping the house clean. If I refused, he hit me."

Sam paused and leaned back on the side of the boat.

Vincent's face wrinkled, his features taut with concern.

"Nathan lost his job, the house, and everything. At that point, we didn't talk, didn't even look at each other anymore. I was nothing to him. At night he'd get violent. So I'd stay away as much as I could. Sometimes I'd just sit outside and read in the cold, waiting until he hopefully went to sleep."

Vincent shook his head. "I sure hate the thought of you shivering in the cold."

Sam nodded. "Hey," attempting to lighten the mood a bit, "maybe that's why I don't mind this Louisiana heat."

His joke didn't ease the pain in his eyes or take the sorrow out of Vincent's.

"When I was seventeen I finally tried to set him straight. One night, I just knew I couldn't stand it anymore. I wasn't going to take it, so I socked him good. He got up and went to the kitchen and came back with a knife. He had the nerve to try to stab me—and I think he would've killed me if he had the chance. Luckily, he was drunk enough that he only cut me a few times on my arms. I fought him off and ran. I came back a few hours later and he was passed out on the floor. That night, I packed up everything I had, which was only a few clothes, and temporarily moved in with a friend. A few weeks after that I was a high school dropout and living on the streets."

Vincent didn't say anything at first, but only looked at him for a moment before speaking. "Makes sense you don't drink, then."

"I wish that was the only reason," Sam said coldly.

He was uncomfortable talking about the painful parts of his life. He tended to hide the hard parts deep in the recesses of his mind, almost pretending they didn't happen. Believing that if he distanced himself from his problems, they seemed less daunting.

Now he felt it was time to bring them into the light.

"Wouldn't you know it, after all I went through, all the years of him drinking, I started drinking myself. I said I'd never turn out to be a monster like him, but there I was, living on the streets and buying booze with every penny I could scrounge. I stayed that way for a few months, constantly in a state of drunkenness and sleeping anywhere I could. Then out of the blue an old lady housed me in her apartment complex for free until I found a job. I almost didn't keep the job because I drank so much. I'd get off of work and drink myself to sleep. That continued for a half year. It took everything I had to sober up—everything. Having money made it hard to quit because it was so easy to buy more. But what helped me finally do it was every time I thought about drinking more, I thought about Nathan and the horrible person he became. That's what ultimately stopped me."

Vincent sighed. "Sam, I'm sorry. I—"

"I don't want you to feel any guilt because you weren't able to keep me," Sam said, interrupting Vincent. "It's not your fault, not mine, nobody's. You never could have known that my life would've ended up that way. Plus, you tried the best you could to get custody of me."

Despite Sam's reassurance, tears streamed down the old man's face. He wiped them from his cheeks. "I'm gonna say it anyway. I'm sorry for you having to go through that. If I ever would've known, you would've been here in Louisiana with me."

"I know, Vin."

Vincent shook his head. "I should have been there for you, took care of you for your parents. What would they have thought if they knew what you had to go through? They always wanted me to be there for you if something happened to them. I tried so hard to get custody of you."

Sam didn't know what to say. He sat back, still looking down at the floor of the boat.

"Maybe that's part of the reason for of all this," Vincent continued. "I want to make up for the years you should've been here. Maybe you came back here so I could help make up for what you had to go through. To tell you about your parents and make everything right."

Sam knew Vincent held some guilt about the situation before, and he could tell that the old man felt it even more so after he'd come clean.

"Vin, it wasn't your fault you couldn't raise me. I know

that. And I didn't tell any of this to hurt you. But I thought I owed it to you to tell you what I've been through. You're the closest thing to family I've got in this world and I owed it to you to let you know who I am."

A fierce expression came across Vincent's face. "That ain't who you are. Don't you ever say that, Sam! You ain't an alcoholic." He hesitated, then asked softly, "But what made you drink after seeing Nathan? Seeing what he did to you?"

Sam's eyes watered and he clenched his fists. "It's just hard going through life without anyone." His tone was one of frustration, and tears started to stream down his face. "I've always felt alone my entire life—abandoned and unwanted. I try to hide it away but it affects me every day."

"You got the best of your parents in you. The absolute best. You really do. I have seen it in you already. You a hard worker and a good person. Don't ever think you a horrible person."

Sam used his shirt to wipe the remaining tears from his eyes. "I like hearing you say that. That helps me look back on all those years and see that maybe I wasn't alone, even though I felt like it at the time."

"That's right, you weren't. Your parents were looking down on you. And ole Vin was here thinking of you, waiting for you to make your way back to Louisiana one day."

Sam had never talked to anyone like this before. The thought that he might be looked upon like a charity case kept him quiet, but he trusted that Vincent wouldn't treat him that way.

No, he thought, as he looked at the old man and wiped the last of his tears away. Vincent would treat him like family.

Eleven

It was the first night Sam would be spending on the house-boat—what he would soon consider his home. After Vincent dropped him off, his skiff sped away into the darkness, his bright light illuminating a pathway through the cypress trees until the noise of the motor grew fainter and the yellow glow disappeared. Sam was quickly surrounded by black. He reached down near the front screen door and picked up the lantern Vincent lent him. He sparked it by twisting a dial on the green, semicircular bottom half and above that, in a glass encasement, a flame appeared.

He walked inside, guided by the lantern, and kicked off his soiled boots and clothes. Parts of his arms were muddy from chasing after bullfrogs all night, but he was too tired to think about cleaning up. All that was on his mind was sleep. He plopped down onto some borrowed blankets on the floor. The thin material wasn't much insulation, yet the crude sleeping surface didn't matter.

Like most every warm night in the Atchafalaya, it was anything but quiet. Cicadas voiced their deafening songs. Owl hoots echoed around the cypress. Bull frogs moaned and groaned, their hums reverberating across the water. Sam thought the sounds were distinctly natural and he liked them—they were easy to get used to. Collectively, the noises weren't abrupt or piercing, rather a gentle and consistent hum. They soothed him as he fell almost immediately to sleep.

Until a loud clatter echoed through the night that wasn't natural.

Sam shot out of slumber, as alert as if he had never fallen asleep. He turned his head to listen for the noise again. Upon sitting up, he caught a glimpse of a light, flashing not far outside the houseboat. He concluded that the noise had been a boat motor revving.

Perhaps Vincent was coming back because he was too tired to drive all the way to his house.

But he looked down at his watch, and it was almost 2:30 a.m. Vincent had left over an hour ago and would have long been back across the levee. Sam knew whoever was near wasn't Vincent.

He sprung from the pallet of blankets as quietly as he could, trying not to cause the old wooden floor to creak under his weight. He struggled to see in the darkness, which, coupled with hazy vision from waking so suddenly, made it hard to contemplate what to do. He stood still to gain composure.

After a moment, he recovered, grabbed a piece of a 2x4 that he felt near his feet, and crept toward the window above the sink. He peered through to see two figures exiting a boat and coming onto the porch. They both had LED lights strapped around their heads, emitting a white beam as they looked all around the houseboat, talking loudly in deep voices. Sam froze and his mind drifted back to his first visit on the houseboat, when Vincent told him of the random thefts that occurred over the years. These two people surely weren't inspecting the work Sam had done on the houseboat earlier in the day. They were there to break in.

The men made their way to the front door. Sam didn't move. He heard one of the intruders open it. He hadn't thought to lock it with the metal latch. Not that it mattered, anyway, as the tattered screen door was hardly a barrier to the outside world. Sam's heart was now pounding wildly. He was unsure what to do and stood motionless, holding the piece of wood in both hands in the dark.

Then, adrenaline took over, as he grabbed the propane light and sparked it, illuminating the room. The two men stopped in their tracks as the space erupted in yellow light. Upon realizing there was a person inside, the man in front reached inside his pants and pulled out a revolver. Sam prepared to rush him, hoping he could pelt him with the block of wood he held, but the second intruder grabbed his partner's hand as the gun was pointed at Sam.

"Hold on!" cried the second man, holding one hand up to Sam while clenching the arm of his partner with his other hand.

"What the hell are you doing here? This is my property," Sam said in a stern tone.

"Put the gun up, man," the second intruder said, a skinny, bald man, sporting a white muscle shirt and blue jeans, to the other.

When his friend, who was also thin-framed, with a pencil-thin goatee and greasy brown hair, complied and lowered the firearm, he turned his attention to Sam. "Look, we ain't here for no trouble. We just ain't never been back here and we saw this houseboat and it didn't look like nobody was here. We were just coming to check it out. We weren't gonna take nothing or anything. You just startled him is all."

Sam kept a tight grip on the plank of wood, his chest heaving, wondering if the man was telling the truth. He decided it would be better to go along with the story for now. Maybe that would get them out of there without a fight.

"I wouldn't advise trespassing on people's property at night, especially with a trigger happy friend." Sam's tone was firm, and he stood his ground near the back room.

The gunman sneered and clenched his fist, with his other hand gripping the silver pistol at his side as he stood next to his friend in the doorway.

"I suggest you both get on your way," Sam boldly continued.

"And that's what we doing," said the second man. "Come on, let's get outta here."

The unarmed man walked out of the doorway and disappeared into the dark of the porch while the gun-wielding intruder lingered and stared at Sam.

"And I suggest you watch how you talk to someone when they holding a gun and you holding a piece of wood, especially this deep in the Basin," the man said.

"You point a gun at my face on my own property and then you threaten me while standing in my house?" Sam said, broadening his shoulders.

The intruder didn't reply; he only stood near the doorway without moving. He and Sam stared back at each other, almost waiting to see which one would strike first. Sam kept his focus on the man's eyes while the frogs and bugs counted the seconds with their blaring voices. The sound of a boat motor outside made the intruder finally break the stare.

He stuck his revolver back into his pants, turned, and silently exited the house, following his companion back onto the boat.

Sam watched them speed off and disappear into the darkness back toward the canal that led to Riley Bayou. He kept watching without moving, staring blankly at the darkness, hoping they wouldn't turn around to sneak up on him when he fell back to sleep.

He stood for a half hour peering into the night before his eyelids again grew heavy. Figuring and hoping it was safe to let his guard down, he fell to the floor, dropping the wood. He took long, almost gasping breaths, as if he had held his breath throughout the entire ordeal. It wasn't the first time he had a gun pointed at him, but a familiarity with the action didn't make it any less dire. But most of all, he couldn't believe the audacity of the man.

Fighting sleep, he processed what could have happened. He acted the only way he knew how, though after the fact, he realized his bravado may have been ill-advised. But what if he had shown his fear? Would the man have gone so easily? Or would he have tried to rob him?

If growing up in a rougher part of Boston taught him anything, it's that when people pushed him, he had to push back. If he didn't, he learned that he would get trampled on. The encounter reminded him that people were the same no matter where he went. If he was in a city of one million or seemingly alone in a swamp, despicable people would always be present, he thought as he drifted to sleep.

The sound of a boat motor woke him. He hadn't moved since he had collapsed to the floor and fallen asleep next to the front door. The sound caused him to jump up and look out the window. In his sleepy deliriousness, he half expected to see the two men back for another round. But it was Vincent walking onto the porch. Sam was slow to stand, and he sluggishly moved to a chair near the kitchen table as he tried to wake up and get his head straight. He had to shake the feeling that what had occurred a few hours prior was only a dream.

Vincent poked his head through the front door. "Good morning, sunshine. Oh, good, you already awake. Though you ain't exactly dressed. I figured I'd get here a little late. Well, if you call an hour after sunrise late."

Sam had his face buried in his hands and didn't look up, not even to address Vincent's quip about him being in his boxers.

"Say, boy, you alright? Frogging got the best of you last night?"

Sam looked up. "Two guys broke in last night not long after you left."

"What?"

"Yeah, and I got a gun pointed in my face."

"You saw who it was? Can you remember what they looked like?" Vincent had a concerned, but irritated look on his face as he walked towards Sam.

"I got a look at them, yeah. But I don't really remember what they looked like in detail. They just looked like normal guys, I guess."

"If I find out who it was I'll whoop both of 'em." Vincent tightened his wrinkled hands into fists.

"If I would've had the boat here they probably wouldn't have come in. Oh, and a deadbolt is on my shopping list."

"And a gun."

Sam sighed. "I don't need a gun out here, Vin. What would've happened if I pulled a gun, too? Then what, we would've shot each other?"

"You need a gun for your protection. Trust me, you don't know what kinda crazy people may come back here."

"I wouldn't even know where to start with a gun. I've never shot one in my life."

"I know it may seem a little scary, but it's a necessity out here. Plus, you'll need one for hunting. No one is telling you that you have to shoot someone with it. But it's always best to have one here just in case you need to use it."

Sam shook his head even though he knew Vincent was right.

"I got a shotgun you can use. It'll be good to keep in here and for when hunting season starts."

"If you say so, Vin. I trust you know better than me what it's like living out here."

"I should've stayed here, though. They are lucky I wasn't," Vincent growled.

"Look, it's OK. I'm alright, they left and they won't be coming back."

"If they do and I'm here, they gonna have something to worry about."

Sam looked up at Vincent and chuckled a bit. "Really, it's fine. I never would've guessed I would've seen someone back here at that time of night. I mean, it was nearly 3 a.m."

"It happens from time to time. They might've been frogging or something. Like I said, this place is secluded, but that don't mean ain't nobody ever gonna come out here."

"Not that I'm justifying the dude pulling a gun, but I can

see why they stopped. This old place looks deserted. They both probably were just curious. That's what the sane guy said, anyway. Just makes me want to get this thing fixed up faster."

"You take getting a gun pointed at you pretty well."

"It isn't the first time, but I hope it's the last. I haven't even been down here a week and I'm already getting into trouble. Has anything like that ever happened to you?"

"Oh yeah it has," Vincent said as he calmed and sat down on a stool across the table from Sam. "That's what I'm saying, it's always best to have a gun, just in case."

"Well, what happened to you?"

"I had people threaten to shoot me several times. They got some crazy Cajuns out here. The last time was a number of years ago when I was alligator hunting. I had gotten a few tags that year and was fishing on a friend's property up near the river. Some guy pulled up to me and accused me of running his lines. I told him I wasn't and he insisted I was. He got pissed off and went to get out a gun. I pulled mine first and told him if he wanted to live he'd stop."

"Good lord, man. That's like some wild west stuff right there."

"You gotta remember, it kinda is like the wild west out here. Not so much like it used to be years ago, but the law doesn't reach far into the Basin. You look out for yourself here, and justice is dished out by the people, not by authorities."

"I guess I didn't realize that."

"It ain't all friendly people out here. I know a majority of them are, but some are rotten, just like you'd find anywhere. Anyway, what'd you say to get them outta here?"

"One of them was reasonable and walked off without me saying much. The guy with the gun, now he was really mad for some reason. I told him he needed to get off of my property. He threatened me, but I stood my ground. He ended up leaving after realizing I wasn't going to back down."

Vincent laughed and slapped the table. "You are your daddy's boy."

"What, did he get guns shoved in his face, too?"

"I don't think he ever went that far. But probably just shy of it. He wasn't afraid of anything, and he always stood up for what he knew was right." Vincent plopped a plastic bag on the table. "Well, on a lighter note. I brought some biscuits from the gas station for breakfast. And I got some of that tin loaded in the boat. So we can get started on the roof. That shouldn't take long at all. And I'm guessing you still up for it, even though it looks like you slept all of five minutes last night."

"Yeah, I'm up for it. I may move a little slower today, but that's not going to stop me."

The men ate quickly, talking about their plans for the day, but part of Sam's mind was preoccupied with the break in. He had a feeling he hadn't seen the last of the man with the gun.

Twelve

It was a crisp November morning and the change in seasons was noticeable, much more so than only a few weeks before. The trees, some of them along the bayou sporting bright red and yellow foliage, were just starting to lose leaves. The days were shorter and the nights chilly, a few of them occasionally hovering just above freezing. Though, in typical Louisiana fashion, any day of the week could yield eighty-degree temperatures. Because of that, the water was still warm and the bugs hadn't gone away for good.

The view of Riley Bayou as Sam guided his boat to check his fishing lines in the ancient skiff that Vincent had given him was different, even though he had made the trip numerous times over the last two months. He had never witnessed so much mist cover the area. The night before had been a cold one, which, combined with the warm water of the Atchafalaya, forced a layer of fog to blanket much of the swamp. He had seen the bayou in so many ways, but a new scene would surprise him every so often. The same imagery periodically had a subtle variance to it: a tree would fall into the bayou; the sun would jet off the clouds at an odd angle; floating vegetation would come in with a current and dot the surface of the water. It kept the familiar view new if he took the time to study it long enough.

Sam pulled up next to a trotline spanning the bayou, around forty yards wide, right next to a bend in the waterway. He pulled off his blue beanie, his long, blond hair twisted in a bun. For the past few months he had neglected to trim it, letting his long locks hang past his shoulders. He peered north down the bayou and struggled to see through the fog. The gray mist was so thick it permeated the trees in the area. He knelt on the edge of the skiff, the cold of the metal seeping through his jeans, and picked up the rope in the water to see what he had on the other end. The first and second hook still had the bait attached. He worked his way down to the other end of the bayou. All of the twelve additional hooks either still contained bait or none at all. The line usually had a few fish on it, enough for breakfast, at least, but today he would have to settle for some store-bought food he kept stashed in the houseboat.

After weeks of observation and practice, he was comfortable catching fish on his own. He could find bait, set lines, and pull in a load of fish with skill. A few times he hauled in more than Vincent. He used jug lines, yo-yos, trotlines, set nets, and cast nets. Sam could butcher a catfish with skill and pull in a load of carp using hoop nets. Then, during the same day, haul in a sack or two of crawfish with pillow traps. He had even learned how to pluck and clean a chicken, which Vincent said was practice for butchering ducks. But more importantly, Vincent taught Sam how to cook every creature that wasn't sold, using Cajun recipes to make dishes like jambalaya, gumbo, and étouffée.

Sam's hands were frigid after dipping them into the water to check his lines. He held them up to his mouth and breathed on them for warmth. Then he drove back to his houseboat, avoiding a faster speed to keep the cold wind from penetrating his hand-me-down, camouflage jacket. The coat swallowed his thin frame. Since his move to Louisiana, he had lost what little fat he had, and replaced it with muscle and a bronze tan.

Just two months living in the bayou state had already changed him, and he owed a lot of it to Vincent. If he had never found him, none of the new life he enjoyed could have been possible. He cared so deeply about Vincent he viewed the old man as a father, and someone who would always be there to guide him. He had never known what it meant to be cared for in such a way, and he finally felt like he was a part of something bigger than himself—part of a family. From day one, and in the most unexpected way, Vincent showed him nothing but compassion and love. Above all, he was thankful beyond words for the opportunity to feel loved—a feeling that had evaded him until now.

As his houseboat came into view, Sam took in the scene with a big smile. No longer did he drift through the weeks, looking at the calendar for a day to pass only to dread the next. He loved every minute he was spending in the Atchafalaya. Most of all, he enjoyed all of the time he was getting to spend in Riley Bayou. Though he wasn't living on the houseboat full-time yet, he did spend most nights there. He saw Vincent at least for a few hours many days, but other than that, his time was spent with only his thoughts and the wilderness around him. It forced him to reflect on his life more than he ever had before. After so many years, he finally felt at ease in his own skin. It was as if all the missing pieces of his life had come together in this strange and wonderful place. When he left Boston he vowed he'd always be grateful for the chance to start a new life in Louisiana. He realized that at that time, he didn't understand the significance of that opportunity. Now he thought that coming to Louisiana wasn't running away as it had first appeared—it was coming home.

Sam bypassed the normal parking spot near the porch of the houseboat and motored to the bank adjacent to his home. On the ridge of nearby high ground, he had cleared the undergrowth to make room for a forthcoming garden, a chicken coop, and an outhouse. But for now he used the area as a workspace to craft pirogues, a skill Vincent had taught him. And just like the old man predicted, Sam learned fast.

The front of his skiff slid up onto the bank and stopped. He rose and walked toward the bow, then stepped out of the boat, his white rubber boots squishing down a few inches into mud. He secured the vessel to a nearby tree with some rope and hurried over to his project, a pirogue he had been working on for Vincent's birthday.

The beauty was twelve feet long and wide enough to make it more stable than most pirogues. Sam wanted to make sure it was safe for Vincent to climb into. It was made from a piece of cypress he had found that sunk in Riley Bayou, from what Vincent had estimated, over a hundred years ago, when loggers had cut down the virgin forest in the area.

Sam found the forgotten behemoth one day when he was fishing. The big chunk of wood had spent so much time resting on the bottom of the bayou that it was stained a golden color.

A little more than two weeks' worth of wood shavings littered the forest floor beneath the saw horses Sam stood in front of. He rubbed the exterior of the pirogue, the first he made on his own, and gave it a gentle pat.

During the crash courses on boat-making that begun not long after the move to Louisiana, Vincent gave Sam all the tricks needed to turn a block of wood into a floating structure. He taught Sam the traditional—and the tougher— way to make the boats, out of an entire block of wood rather than using thin, pre-cut lumber. The whole block of wood had to be measured and cut to the desired length and height without error. Then, the inside had to be chipped with an axe or burned away with hot coals, a process that required an intensely meticulous approach that could take many days. It was a tricky art to ensure the pirogue was buoyant enough to not sink with added weight while also having a sound design structurally.

Sam had tried to make a few throughout his lessons with Vincent, but could never perfect the process—though he came close. The first prototype didn't float because he con- structed the sides too shallow. The second he measured in- correctly and ended up cutting too much wood out of the inside, which compromised the structural integrity. Although Sam had never worked much with tools previously, he found out that he was good at working with his hands. Almost since day one in Louisiana, he was building something or using his hands on a daily basis. He liked the hard work, and being able to see the progression of a project that he undertook. Working with wood, especially when it came to building the pirogues, challenged him, and he enjoyed having to figure out what to do next to get it just right.

As Sam inspected the design some more, he was proud that he hadn't messed up once. He used the woodworking skills he picked up over the last few weeks from working with Chris to build a camp near Bayou Pigeon, as well as his own projects to fix up his houseboat. The superior craftsmanship on the pirogue was noticeable from first glance. It was cut and shaped just like he wanted it, the bottom perfectly flat. The bow had a sharp point, the middle was wide for stability and the stern shaped, like the front, at a sharp angle. It had two seats, one in the front and one at the rear, and an open middle for storage. Sam smiled as he looked at it resting above the forest floor.

He knelt down and picked up a quart of black paint. He shook it and set it on the ground, popping it open with a flathead screwdriver. A nearby stick served to continue mixing up the paint before he began. His fingers curled around an aged brush, and he dipped it in the bucket.

He carefully painted the words *'famille, amour, une vie'* on the side of the pirogue. He stood back to examine the penmanship, which elicited a smile. At first he didn't truly understand what his mother meant by the phrase, but now he knew. The words were more to him than letters. It was a way of life. It was something intangible that he'd strive for every day.

He felt it when he looked at Vincent. He felt it when he looked at a photograph of his parents. He felt it, more than anywhere else, in Riley Bayou.

Thirteen

Vincent sat at a fold-up table in his backyard while Chris tended to a barbeque pit. Sam watched over a pot of sizzling grease sitting atop a burner fueled by propane. The three men were gathered next to the covered porch where Vincent butchered fish and wild game at the rear of the old shack, just before the jumbles of scraps that filled the rest of the cleared part of the property.

Most days when the three got together, Vincent was the chef. The old man usually insisted upon it. Sam and Chris didn't complain, especially since Vincent had quite the knack for serving up some quality Cajun fare. He made meals from recipes passed down to him from his mother and father, which were passed down to them by their parents. Boudin, cracklin, crawfish étouffée, gumbo, and jambalaya were the old man's specialties.

Of course, he was quite fond of frying almost anything he could, from squirrels to frogs and fish to deer.

Sam had always figured the way to make a Cajun dish was to add pepper to give it a kick. Vincent schooled him otherwise, showing him the Cajun holy trinity—bell peppers, onions, and celery—that gave a Cajun meal its flavor.

For once, the old man wasn't the one cooking dinner since he was the guest of honor, but that didn't stop him from giving his two cents whenever he could.

"You need more cayenne pepper," Vincent shouted over from his chair to Chris, who was seasoning a few slabs of deer tenderloins.

"Just sit back and drink your beer, you old man," Chris casually quipped.

Vincent was turning seventy-eight just a week before Thanksgiving. The old man's rough exterior was deceptive, and he looked a decade older, thanks to his years spent working under the sun that turned his face dark and leathery, most of it hidden by his bushy beard.

"Make sure not to overdo those frog legs," Vincent said as Sam dipped the battered meat into boiling grease. Vincent stood and walked up to the pot, and turned the dial on the burner. "You had it a little hot, boy. Gonna burn them things."

Chris shook a pair of tongs at Vincent. "Sit your butt down. You the guest of honor and you not supposed to be doing nothing. Let that boy cook them legs, he'll be alright."

Sam shook his head and laughed. "Do you two ever quit teasing one another?"

"Well, if y'all would be cooking the right way I wouldn't have to tease no body." Vincent said, his near toothless grin barely visible under his beard.

There wasn't anyone else coming to celebrate with them that fall afternoon. Chris and Sam were the extent of the old man's close friends. Vincent had a few other casual acquaintances around town, but for the most part, he was a quiet man who kept to himself and that was the way he liked it. The only family he had left was a brother in Kansas, but the two didn't talk much anymore. His brother, Tony, had moved away after coming back from Europe after World War II to take a job in Topeka. He'd found a wife and had lived there ever since. Vincent hadn't seen him in more than fifteen years, since he never strayed far outside of the Atchafalaya other than his time spent in the Army.

Smoke rose from the homemade, black barbeque pit as Chris opened it and flipped over the tender deer meat with tongs. Vincent had welded the bulky, square pit together more than twenty years ago, and even though it wasn't the best looking thing, the square design heated up well and regulated the temperature even better; it was a good thing for Chris who was trying to keep the lean meat medium rare to ensure it didn't turn tough and dry.

Much like his skiff, Vincent boasted of the pit almost every time he used it, and this day was no exception.

Chris inspected the slabs of meat, poking them over with a knife. "I think these might be about done."

"It's about time," Vincent said with a smirk as he smoked one of his signature hand-rolled cigarettes and sipped on a light beer.

Sam was still preoccupied with frying the frog legs, a process Vincent had taught him not long ago. He hoped he wasn't messing up the timing of how long the meat needed to sizzle in the grease. But he was fairly certain he'd gotten the spices right, although Vincent's seasoning recipe was exhaustive and hard to remember. It involved several types of spices, mustard, eggs, and a slew of other ingredients.

"You're lucky you're even turning seventy-eight with all this healthy food you eat," Sam said with a tone of sarcasm.

He was never one to cook fried foods all that often, but that changed quickly after he spent time with Vincent.

"That's the secret to living a long life, boy. How you think I'm in such good shape," Vincent said, holding his stomach.

After dinner was finished and their conversation started to dwindle, Sam saw a chance to present Vincent with the pirogue. He got up from the log he had been sitting on. "Chris, you mind coming to help me in your truck for just a second?"

Chris stood and covertly winked at Sam. "Yeah, sure thing." He followed Sam toward the front of the house.

"Where y'all going?" Vincent asked, his feet propped up as he lounged in a chair.

"Don't worry about it. We'll be right back," Chris shouted as they rounded the corner and disappeared out of sight.

"Man, you did a hell of a job with this thing. You really did. You could sell something like this for a good chunk of change," Chris said as he examined the pirogue in the bed of his green, single cab pickup. Earlier in the day, Sam had transported the pirogue to the landing and passed it off to Chris so they could ferry it to Vincent's house.

"Thanks, I appreciate it. And it even floats. Trust me, I checked several times this week to make sure."

The two men unloaded the surprise present and carried it above their heads toward Vincent's backyard. The solidly built structure was heavier than Sam wanted it to be. Vincent would likely have to obtain help loading it into the bed of his truck when he wanted to use it.

When Sam and Chris rounded the corner of the house

with the pirogue, Vincent looked up and his eyes widened. "Whoa, what y'all got there?" he said, getting up from his chair.

Chris and Sam laid the boat on the ground near Vincent's feet.

"Well, what do you think?" Sam asked.

"You made this?"

"I surely didn't buy it at Home Depot. Of course I made it for you. Happy birthday, Vin."

A wide grin was visible through Vincent's gray beard, and he slowly bent down to get a closer look at the pirogue. He rubbed it gently on its side and walked around it twice, inspecting its craftsmanship closely. He walked over to Sam and hugged him, wrapping both of his hands firmly across Sam's back. When he stepped back, he had a tear rolling down his cheek. "Sam, this is the nicest thing anyone has ever given me. I absolutely love it."

"It was the least I could do for you, Vin. For all you've done for me."

"We gonna have to go take this thing out soon. And it's even got your momma's saying on it. That's a nice touch."

Sam smiled at the old man's visible excitement about the present. "I figured you'd like that."

"It looks so well made. How long you been working on this thing for?"

"I guess about two weeks. I've been putting in time on it every afternoon."

Vincent smiled and shook his head while he rubbed Martha's phrase on the side of the pirogue.

Chris shifted a cake onto the table and chimed in. "Well, how about we eat some cake? Now, this ain't no pirogue, but

I made this thing last night and it took me two tries."

Vincent glanced over at the sheet cake in a glass pan. "That's a cake out a box. How you messed that up?"

"Hey, I ain't no baker, OK?" Chris said.

Sam laughed while he cut the cake into pieces. He served Vincent and Chris before he, too, had a sliver.

"This ain't so bad," Vincent said with a mouthful.

"Yeah, it's pretty good," added Sam.

Chris sniffed the cake and hesitantly took a bite. "Wow, this is a lot better than my first try."

More conversation followed after they'd eaten the cake, persisting well into the night, until Chris retired to his trailer near the Bayou Pigeon landing. Sam and Vincent moved inside to get out of the cold. The old shack wasn't much warmer than outside, though it did work to block out the wind. Vincent had a lone propane heater positioned in the corner of the first room, which barely sent any heat radiating toward them.

Sam thought it wasn't good for the old man to be staying in such a chilly place all the time. He decided he'd have to work on the fireplace, which wasn't structurally sound and thus unusable.

They sat around the kitchen table, like they always did to talk, but they both still donned their camouflage jackets to keep warm. Vincent sipped on a beer instead of a cup of coffee and had tobacco scattered across the table while he prepared to roll a cigarette. His old, yellowing fingernails scraped the tobacco together as he talked. "So, tomorrow is the big day, huh? You finally moving out into the Basin for good."

"That's right. I figure I've finally got enough renovations done to stay there all the time now. I'll take all of that furniture tomorrow morning, just one load should do it, and I'll be set." Sam had compiled furniture from various places, a majority of it from a local fisherman's garage sale, and stashed it inside Vincent's small shack in anticipation of the move.

"You know, you gonna have to get a truck sooner or later, too."

"That's right. I can't keep relying on you for rides all the time. Come to think of it, I've hardly been outside of Bayou Pigeon since I got here. I wouldn't even know where to start looking."

"There's a dealership in Plaquemine."

"I guess that's the next thing on the list. Don't know how I'll afford that, but it's something I'll have to do." Sam scooted forward in his chair and looked at Vincent, his face more serious than before. "Look, Vin, I know I've told you this already, but thank you so much for everything over the past few months. I honestly don't know if you could've helped any more than you have."

Vincent shook his head and leaned back in his chair. "And I said many times before, you family, and that's how we take care of family down here."

"You really are my family. I've never had anyone in my life I could call a father. You're it. I look up to you as a role model, you know."

Vincent lit his freshly rolled cigarette with a match. He took a long, deep drag and exhaled. "Man, I wish we could've been doing this for years, visiting and fishing together, but I guess I don't know how life would have ended up if you would've stayed down here with me. Since you been back, I think about it a lot. Your life would've been so different."

Vincent paused. He puffed again on his cigarette while he tried to find the right words. "You would've been like my son. But, either way, I think the end result has been the same. You exactly who you would've been if you would've never left Louisiana. You a smart young man, got a good head on your shoulders. You still like a son to me. All of this has made me a happy ole man. It's given me something to look forward to in my ole age. I just wish I could've seen you grow up all those years and known you for longer."

"At least we're getting the time we have now, you know? I've been thinking about that, too. Like, what are the odds that you still lived in Bayou Pigeon when I came looking for you?"

"Ain't that the truth? I never, in a million years, would have thought I would see you again, but I hoped like hell that I would. When you first pulled up down my driveway those few months ago, it took everything I had in me to not run up to you and grab you, hug you, and cry. You know that? I held myself together."

"Well, after you decided not to shoot me, right?"

Vincent roared with laughter. "What was I to expect with a city slicker coming down my driveway in a little bitty ole car?"

Sam stuck both hands in his jacket pockets to warm them. Talking about that day made him reflect on how far he'd come.

"I think one of the main things I've learned these past few months is that you can't change the past and you can't run away from it. Regretting certain things about it won't change the present or future, either. I don't resent my child-hood anymore. I don't particularly like it, but it is what it is. I've accepted that now. What I'm happy about is how life is now. I am here and that's all that matters."

"You don't have any regrets?"

"I don't regret anything about my life—nothing. Not anymore. You know, I thought being here, I'd start a new life and never have to think about Boston ever again. I figured I'd be away from that part of my life and it would just fade away. But I've begun to realize that no matter where you go, your life follows you. Just because you're somewhere new doesn't mean what you've been through disappears. You were right that being in this swamp would help me confront my issues. I've come to find that I'd rather accept my past rather than flee it. I've even been trying to find the strength to forgive Nathan for what he did all those years ago. I'm still working on that part, though."

"That's a brave and mature thing to do, Sam. It really is."

"Well, I know that continuing to hold hatred in my heart for Nathan won't do anything for me. After all of the silent meditation I've been doing I've had an opportunity to grow in many ways. I came here for answers about my parents and it's morphed into the chance for me to discover a lot about myself."

"That's good, boy, that's good. Speaking of your parents, I been wanting to ask you if you feel like you got what you came for," Vincent said as he crushed another beer can with his hand and tossed it into the trash.

"Like did I get my questions about them answered?"

"Sure."

"Well, I'm sure I'll always have questions, but yeah. For starters, I know what they look like now. I think I've stared at their pictures so much that I could paint you a picture of them. And speaking of, I've been thinking of learning to paint like my mother."

"That would be nice. I know she would have liked that."

"Yeah, I thought so. I guess now I see them more as they actually existed, if that makes any sense."

"How's that?"

"Before I never had any proof they ever lived. All I had were names from someone telling me these were my parents. I didn't know for sure. Not until I came here and I discovered everything about them was I able to feel like it was all real. The pictures, the houseboat, you—it all makes them more than just an idea I held in my head when I was a kid. It makes it reality."

"Ole Vin can understand that."

"And even though I don't ever remember seeing them, being in Riley Bayou, I feel like I am with them almost every day. While I'm in Riley Bayou and on the houseboat, I know they are never far away. That's one of the reasons I was drawn to that houseboat. I knew I could feel them there with me. And it's beyond just the bayou. I feel them when I'm in the Atchafalaya. I don't even know if I can describe the feeling when I say I can feel them. But there's just something inside me that feels right when I'm out there. Something that's whispering reassurances to me, making me feel at peace."

Vincent stubbed out his cigarette and exhaled the last of the smoke. "Vin's felt like that for years. Going back in that ole houseboat, especially now that you fixed it up like you have, brings me back thirty years to when your parents owned it."

"When I'm out there, I can feel time slowing. It's like I'll spend almost a week out there and when I come back to all the cars and people at the boat launch, it feels like I've been gone a month. Life is only as fast as you live it inside the Basin."

Vincent leaned closer to Sam across the table. "You really are shaping into a regular Cajun." The old man grabbed the box of matches on the table. "I can't tell the difference between you and your daddy anymore."

"You think so?"

"Of course. I even am starting to sense a little Cajun accent creeping in when you talk."

Sam laughed. "I bet so, hanging out with you and Chris all the time. You know how long it took me to figure out what you were saying one hundred percent of the time?"

Vincent grinned with a freshly rolled cigarette held firmly between his lips.

"It's been great, though," Sam continued. "I'm loving my life here. I'm looking forward to living in the Atchafalaya full time. It's an adventure like I've never had before. Do you think I'm ready?"

"You are more than ready. You got everything it takes and you gonna do fine."

Fourteen

Sam and Vincent had filled every square inch of Sam's boat with furniture and supplies, leaving only a small space near the rear. After the last item was secured in the bow with a strap, Sam climbed over everything carefully to make his way to the stern while the boat rocked in the water.

Vincent stood on the muddy bank of the Intracoastal Canal peering at Sam maneuver over and around the jumble in the boat. The old Cajun wore a green and black plaid jacket and khaki overalls with plenty of insulation. Like usual, a cigarette shook in his mouth as he spoke. "You sure you ain't gonna need any help getting all of this in there?"

Sam crawled into the only free space near the outboard motor. As he stood he said, "I got it, really. You just relax today and enjoy it. After I get all of this inside and situated, if I've got enough time, I'm thinking of making a duck hunt." Sam started the outboard motor and it roared to life.

Vincent's bushy eyebrows raised. "First solo hunt?"

"Wish me luck." The first time Sam fired the shotgun Vincent loaned him was on a morning squirrel hunt a few weeks earlier. He proved to be a horrible shot, only managing to hit leaves and branches. "If I bag a few I'll cook them up for supper and you can come by. But even if I come home empty handed, I'll be cooking anyway."

"Alright, I'll do that then. When you thinking?"

"Probably an hour or so before dark. Sound good?"

"I'll be there."

Sam started reversing away from the shore and out into the canal. "OK," he shouted. "Hey, thanks again for helping me get all of this loaded in here this morning, Vin. I'll see you this afternoon."

Vincent waved before walking back past the willow trees lining the canal and to the parking lot. Sam turned his attention to driving, cautiously taking off toward Little Bayou Pigeon. It was hard for him to see the bayou ahead with all his belongings piled higher than the sides of the boat. Any sudden turns could have possibly capsized the top-heavy vessel, which had surely seen its better days. The old outboard motor Vincent had given him to fasten to the boat was struggling to get going with all of the added weight, so he made sure to keep to a leisurely pace.

After an hour of slowly maneuvering his boat through the Atchafalaya, he pulled in through the cypress guarding the entry to Riley Bayou. When he caught sight of the house-boat's yellow exterior he smiled. A few weeks ago he added a green trim along the top and bottom of the walls, as well as green posts, to accentuate the bright color. He also painted his mother's adage in big, black cursive letters on the wall facing the outer part of the bayou. He couldn't shake the urge to smile again as he caught sight of it.

The whole process had been tough, and he still had a few projects left to do, but he was enjoying every moment. He relished pushing his limits, mentally and physically, as he worked on projects. Over the last few months he had come to understand firsthand the Cajun ingenuity that Vincent so often talked about. If he didn't know how to fix something during the renovation process, he didn't have anyone to call. Besides, cell service was non-existent in many places, anyway, even if Vincent would've had a phone. So he relied on what he had learned from the old man and Chris, as well as his own creativity, to attempt to resolve whatever issues came up on his own.

It took the entire morning to load all of the furniture into the houseboat and arrange it just like he wanted. Normally, he'd be working up quite a sweat, but the early season cold front that came through the night before kept the temperatures in the 40s until noon. The cold, cloudy morning made for a pleasant time to work.

A double bed was set up in the middle of the bright, baby blue bedroom, with a bookcase and a small lamp at its foot against the wall. The tiny room was just big enough to walk by comfortably on both sides of the bed. The bookcase was fastened out of boards of sinker cypress, a house-warming gift made by Chris. Sam stacked a few books on it that he intended to read in his spare time during the winter, among them "Walden" by Henry David Thoreau and "My First Summer in the Sierra" by John Muir. The tattered books had belonged to his father. Being engulfed in nature turned out to be something Sam loved immensely, a trait he figured he got from his father. Nature aided Sam's process of self-discovery, a journey he felt he was continuing every day, and he was looking forward to reading the thoughts of people who felt the same way.

In the main room, near the entrance to the bedroom,

was a small sofa he bought at the garage sale. He had a small coffee table positioned just in front of the couch. Along the same wall, he set up the kitchen table and two chairs located closer to the front door. The small table had belonged to his parents, and it had somehow survived a flood and countless thieves. He refinished it with the same aged oak stain he had applied to the cabinets.

Despite the minimal belongings, the place didn't look bare. The little houseboat filled up quickly.

Sam tossed a dozen of Vincent's mallard decoys into the bow of his skiff just after he arranged the last of the furniture. He also threw in a pair of waders that would shield him from water all the way up to his mid-chest. He knew this particular day would be a good one for duck hunting in the Atchafalaya due to the cold front and cloudy weather. Vincent had told him that waterfowl migrated to south Louisiana ahead of cold fronts, down from northern states as far up as North Dakota and into Canada, during the fall and winter.

He took off to his hunting grounds, just up Riley Bayou and off the main channel. He drove north and turned down a small, cypress-lined slough. The waterway, only fifteen yards wide, was full of sunken trees, so he drove slowly to avoid hitting any with the propeller of his motor. The needle-like leaves of the cypress in the area were a burnt orange color, a stark contrast from the Spanish moss that covered the branches. The clouds blocking much of the sunlight gave the colors a dull appearance that day, but Sam knew how handsomely bright the leaves were, having seen them in full sun only a few days prior.

The slough connected to a small lake with a few cypress trees growing up out of the water here and there. He drove into the middle of the lake and threw out the dozen decoys, not far from a cluster of cypress that he thought would serve as his makeshift duck blind, and a perfect hiding spot.

He peered at his decoys from inside the boat, and shoved three red shotgun shells into his gun. His neck was adorned with two duck calls that hung on a lanyard. Vincent had showed Sam how to use the calls, but Sam had trouble during the practice sessions. He could never mimic the right cadence to sound quite like a duck. He figured he'd keep the calling to a minimum in order to not scare the prey away.

An hour passed and Sam hadn't seen many birds fly overhead. He had called at a group of ducks earlier to no avail.

Then, he saw a low-flying group of birds zooming over the trees to his left. He could instantly tell they were ducks by the way they flew. Their necks stretched out ahead and their wings flapped hurriedly. There were maybe five or six in total. He couldn't tell exactly what kind they were at this point, but he suspected that perhaps they were wood ducks or one of the species of teal. Maybe even mallards.

Regardless, Sam picked up his mallard call, one that he knew appealed to most duck species, and blew into it three times in quick succession. He thought it actually didn't sound half bad that time. He stopped to see if the birds thought so, too. Apparently they did and they all dipped below the tree line, circling back around the lake, before they started heading straight toward him.

They were nearly eighty yards away before Sam realized he needed to prepare for a shot. The tiny black dots flew in tandem and matched each other's moves as they closed the distance between themselves and the cluster of cypress trees

Sam hid in. The sight of them approaching sent Sam's heart fluttering uncontrollably. He slowly inched his shaking pointer finger toward the trigger to flick off the safety. He barely breathed as he gripped the shotgun against his chest to prepare to shoot.

The ducks were upon him before he could even think to move. They landed in the water next to his decoys only thirty yards away. He raised his gun, and the ducks, having spotted the movement, shot back off into the air almost as soon as they landed, flapping their wings frantically as water kicked up in every direction. Sam didn't know which duck to shoot at first.

His first shot was placed in the middle of the pack of six. It didn't meet its mark. He was quickly losing his chance to bag one of the animals as they floated higher into the air to escape the danger. His second shot, he aimed at the last bird in the pack. Another miss. He pumped the gun to reload his last shell into the chamber and again aimed at the last duck in the group. He held his breath, closed his left eye, placed the tip of the barrel right above where the duck was flying, and pulled the trigger. The duck somersaulted in the air and folded, losing its upward trajectory and falling from the sky. It plopped in the water with a splash as Sam looked on from his perch in the cypress trees.

"Alright!" he exclaimed, his shout echoing across the lake.

The other five ducks continued their escape into the distance as Sam held up a fist in a celebratory fashion. He trudged up to the duck floating in the water; it was a blue-winged teal, the smallest of the dabbling ducks, and a male, with a brown body, dark head and a white line across its cheek. He was proud of the clean and ethical shot he made. He was also pleased that he would have a duck to cook for Vincent that night.

He returned to the blind for another hour and called at a few other groups of ducks that flew near the lake, but no others came into shooting range. With around three hours of daylight left he figured it was time to head back home to butcher his prize.

Sam finished preparing dinner just as the sun was setting. He took the food inside to escape the chill. He peered out of the window for a sign of Vincent, but couldn't see clearly anymore. Night had fallen and it was bitterly cold for Louisiana standards. It was again going to dip below freezing that night and it was already likely in the 30s. With the wind chill it was forecasted to feel more like the mid-20s.

While he waited for Vincent, he occupied his time by putting the finishing touches on a few details of his home. He hung three of his mother's paintings in the main room: one of a sunset near the front door, a faded portrait of his father over the sofa, and one of Vincent in the bedroom right over the bookcase. He also decorated the bookcase with photographs of his parents and Vincent. He organized his clothes in the closet, which also doubled as a bathroom. By the time he was done the old man still hadn't shown up. So he ate the cold meat and scarfed down a few biscuits. He figured Vincent must have had something going on to cause him to be late.

He wished the old man had a cell phone.

After eating, he relaxed on the sofa with the copy of "Walden." He had a small butane heater situated near his feet providing him just enough warmth to keep cozy. He covered up with a blanket and despite his tiredness, began reading through Thoreau's most widely known work. It was the first time Sam had enough free time to read it, but it had been months since he read anything.

The first sentence of the novel was underlined, which immediately piqued his interest. He flipped through several other pages to find that his father had underlined passages. He turned back to the first page of the book and lost himself in Thoreau's words.

It was almost as if Thoreau was speaking to him through the pages. The author had moved into a secluded cabin to simplify his life and become acquainted with nature. It was a theme that resonated with Sam, and apparently his father. He understood Ryan's interest in wanting to leave behind civilization for the solace of nature. Solitude and the tranquility of the wilderness were necessities of life, Thoreau wrote— and Sam wholeheartedly agreed. He began reading with a deliberate vigor to comprehend the 19th century literary prose, as well as to commit the poetic phrases to memory that his father had underlined. The poetic verses ran throughout his head, as he compared his own experiences with the wilderness of the Basin.

He began to understand the powerful effect nature could have on the human psyche not long after he started spending alone time in Riley Bayou. It wasn't just the trees, the fresh air or the sound of the birds—it was all of it, and much more. It was a quiet, such an immense quiet, that he felt like he could hear his own heartbeat; though it was, at times, indescribable, he even felt a spiritual calmness that made him think with clarity. Time, most days, wasn't important. He wasn't a slave to a watch or a schedule. The sun and the weather dictated his days. He was a part of nature and nature was a part of him—the two were inseparable. He lived not as a visitor to the wild but among it, the end result of a pivotal period of growth.

He underlined a passage that stood out to him, and lost himself in thoughts of his father reading Thoreau's words, forgetting that Vincent had yet to arrive for dinner.

Fifteen

Sam woke up early the next morning, lying on the couch, just as the sun was starting to peak over the horizon. He still gripped his copy of "Walden." Squinting in the dim light, he reached down to the floor and grabbed a box of matches, sparked one, and lit a candle he had stashed nearby.

He mustered the energy to unravel the blankets that lay over him, exposing him to the frigid temperature that had engulfed the houseboat. Even with a heater running all night, it was cold enough that each time he exhaled, a vapor was visibly billowing out of his mouth and nostrils.

Guided by candlelight, he made a cup of instant coffee to warm his body and sat at the table, ready to finish the rest of the duck and biscuits he had cooked the previous night. But at the first sight of the food, he was struck with the realization that Vincent had never showed up.

Sam froze, a biscuit halfway to his mouth. What if something happened to him? Terrible scenarios began to paint themselves in Sam's mind, and he put down his food and poked his head out of the newly installed wooden front door, opening the screen door, and watched as his breath streamed out into the morning air.

A thermometer that hung near the front door showed it was twenty-eight degrees. A white layer of frost covered the swamp, clinging to the branches of trees and blanketing the ground that looked like a drizzling of snow from the night before. He had hoped he would see Vincent motoring up in his skiff, waving and grinning, but the water was still and there was no distant sound of an approaching boat. Sam pulled back into the house and tried to think about what to do. Part of him screamed to go and jump in his boat to check on the old man, while another part tried to calm his frantic mind, insisting that Vincent's absence was most likely due to something benign, and that he obviously couldn't call to tell Sam because he had no phone.

Sam shrugged, deciding he'd quell his worries for a spell, giving Vincent a few hours to show up. But he needed to at least keep himself occupied while he waited, to keep his mind from wandering. He decided he'd start work on the walkway like he planned, which would lead from his porch across the water to the ridge of high ground.

After donning a thick set of clothing, he set to work. He started laying the 2x4 pieces of wood he had cut at Vincent's to serve as the foundation of the walkway.

Though he was consumed with the work, his mind wandered anyway. He couldn't shake the thought of Vincent not showing up, and he wondered where the old man could be. Lost? No way, he thought, Vincent knew the bayous better than anyone. Hurt? Hopefully not, plus Vincent was a tough one. Sam concluded that Vincent was visiting with Chris, perhaps too wrapped up in a good conversation to have made it yet. Telling himself that helped to calm his nerves until he finished his work.

After Sam positioned the foundation, one end sitting atop the houseboat porch and the other resting on the high ground, the work turned into a routine. He would lay a board down on top of the foundation, nail at each corner and repeat, stacking them close together with a hair of a crack. In just an hour, the walkway was almost complete. But he didn't have all of the boards with him to finish. Vincent was supposed to bring the rest of the lumber when he had come over the previous night. Again, the thoughts of the old man's absence consumed him.

He walked inside, grabbed a bigger coat and a beanie, and hopped in his boat. The sound of the motor broke through the quiet. He had enough. He was going to look for Vincent.

He drove east down Little Bayou Pigeon at a brisk pace, his face hidden under a scarf. It was still early, just shy of 8 a.m., and temperatures were still hovering around the upper 30s. His thick jacket, combined with thermal underwear, wasn't enough to completely seal out the chilly wind.

When he pulled up to the landing he parked near a floating dock and tied up his boat. He stopped before walking across the walkway that led to dry land, a familiar vehicle catching his eye. Vincent's truck with the trailer behind it was parked in the old man's normal space.

Sam's heart dropped.

He climbed back into his boat and drove in the direction where he had just come from. Instead of going back to Riley Bayou he started toward Chris' camp, hoping Vincent had stopped off there before checking traps.

The drive to Grand Lake wasn't as easy for Sam to remember as all of the other routes. Some days he had to turn around or consult a map to get to the lake. He hoped today wouldn't be one of those days.

Just the same, he did get turned around once, and he swore at himself, gritting his teeth. There wasn't time for mistakes like that.

As he exited the mouth of Big Bayou Pigeon, the water-way that connected to Grand Lake, Sam headed south toward Chris' island camp. Sam glanced up toward the sky upon entering the lake to see flocks of snow geese, formed in a neat 'v' pointed toward the Gulf of Mexico. The sight reminded him that he and Vincent had a waterfowl hunt planned just a few days ahead. They were supposed to camp near the mouth of the Atchafalaya River hunting geese to serve on Thanksgiving. He had been looking forward to this trip for weeks, but now the thought of it only dampened his spirits further.

When Sam rounded the edge of the slender island, he saw Chris' boat but not Vincent's. He pulled up and moored anyway, hoping that Chris knew something about his where-abouts.

Sam walked across the long pier and up the stairs to the camp, knocked a few times on Chris' front door, and barged in. Though Sam had seen Chris in his underwear one too many times, he was too antsy to ask about Vincent to care.

Chris sat shirtless, scarfing down a bowl of cereal at the table. "What's up, dude? You finished moving in?" he asked, milk dripping from his lip down to his chin.

"Vincent was supposed to come over yesterday, but never showed up."

Chris quit chewing his cereal and set the bowl down on the table. "Wait, so he never went to your house yesterday?"

"No he never came by."

"He came by yesterday around lunch. When he left he said he was heading to your house."

"Is there anywhere you think he might be?"

Chris blinked a few times and shook his head. "I...I don't think so," he stumbled.

Sam's eyes widened, and his stomach churned. He could feel himself becoming frantic. "We've got to go look for him." He burst out the door and ran down the stairs.

"Wait, I'm right behind you," Chris shouted as he ran out of the camp, struggling to get into a coat and pull on some leather boots.

Sam quickly untied his boat from Chris' pier. He jumped in the skiff and cranked the motor. "I'll look around Murphy Lake to see if he is around there checking traps or something. I'll work my way back up to you." He reversed away from the pier and began to turn.

"OK. I'll check the north side of the lake and near the river," Chris said as he pulled on his clothes. "I'll go over to Bayou Chene, too. He's been talking about going over there to see an old friend recently."

"Let's meet at the landing at eleven. If I'm not there call 9-1-1."

Sam zoomed out of the cove of the island and retraced his route from just a few minutes ago, back toward the eastern levee and Murphy Lake. He pushed his motor to its limit, throttling the handle to the max. The outboard whined as it zipped through the water at speeds up to 50 mph. The crisp morning air beat against the parts of Sam's face not covered by the scarf. He didn't care, because his entire body already felt numb.

He navigated through the turns to exit Grand Lake, and made the right turns without hesitation or thinking of where he needed to go—it was instinctual.

He thought about his parents as he drove. And he thought about Vincent relaying his parent's accident to him, how his father was an experienced fisherman who knew where every stump and obstacle was in all the bayous, and how he still succumbed to the wildness of the Atchafalaya. Sam played all the scenarios through his head: Vincent hit a stump and drowned or an alligator pulled the old man in the water. Sam shook his head to rid the thoughts from his mind.

Vincent was fine, he thought—he had to be.

Sixteen

S am peered at each side of the cypress-lined bayou, frantically scanning the banks as fast as he could. His mind
raced. His eyes shot in every direction. The tightness in his
chest only intensified. His heart fluttered uncontrollably, no
matter how many times he attempted to calm himself.

Vincent is fine, he's just around the corner, he thought.
But the more he repeated the line, the less he believed it.

When he entered Murphy Lake he took a right and
scoured every inch of the shore and the line of traps he remembered Vincent showing him, as well as each spot he
thought the old Cajun could be. His heart sank further when
he rounded the lake and was back where he started without
finding any clues. It had taken him almost a half hour to
search the lake. Since leaving Chris' camp he had already
spent an hour searching with nothing to show for it. It was
taking too long. He figured if something had happened to
Vincent he needed to call a rescue team in case the old man
needed help. If Vincent had fallen in the water he could be
grappling with hypothermia, a stress the old man's heart
wouldn't take well.

He continued to try not to panic and keep the negative thoughts at bay, even as he told himself Vincent was only fishing. No, maybe he was hunting or riding down bayous like he often did. Yeah, he thought, that's it. The old man is probably wrapping up a duck hunt and will have a few ducks to cook for supper.

Sam decided there were a few other nearby spots he needed to check before making the call to Chris. He sped out of the lake and took a sharp left, taking a shortcut toward Catfish Lake near Riley Bayou.

He scanned the bank as best as he could while driving as fast as possible. When he would pass near a small lake, he'd check for any signs of the old man's skiff. He did that three times before approaching a large section of cypress. He almost passed the area up, fearing the water level might've been too low for his boat to make it through. But he made a right turn anyway to swing through. The lake turned toward the north before it came to a dead end. Almost as soon as he made the turn he spotted Vincent's boat floating in the middle of the lake. And in it, he spotted Vincent, sitting near the rear.

Sam's worry dissipated, and he heaved a sigh of relief. He ran his trembling hands through his hair and breathed a deep, much needed gulp of air. He motored over toward Vincent to rib the old man. He figured Vincent would get a kick out of him and Chris getting so worried. If anything annoyed Vincent, it was someone trying to do something for him or treat him "elderly," like he would often say.

As Sam got closer to the skiff, something didn't seem right. Vincent didn't move or look to see who was approaching, but continued to just sit there, slouching forward.

"Vin," Sam shouted loudly above the noise of his motor as he approached. Still, Vincent didn't move or respond. As Sam got next to the boat, he looked over at the old man and knew right away.

Sam cupped his mouth, losing whatever breath he had just gained back. He stood in his boat parallel to Vincent's, unable to move. He couldn't think. He couldn't do anything. Time stood still as he stared at his mentor and best friend sitting motionless on the milk crate, leaned against the outboard motor, just feet from him. Vincent was propped up with a slight slouch, preventing him from falling sideways into the bottom of the skiff. The old man was wearing a flannel jacket and a gray wool hat. He had the rest of the wood that Sam needed for the walkway piled in the boat. He had his gun packed, too, probably to join Sam for the duck hunt the day before.

Sam stared at Vincent without emotion, as if he didn't believe what he was witnessing. As if he hoped that the old man was just playing a prank or taking a nap. Sam waited for him to wake up at any second, and burst out laughing like he was so prone to do, and then start puffing on a cigarette. But Vincent's head, tilted down, his beard dangling down to his lap, didn't budge. His pale, purplish face remained motionless.

Sam climbed into Vincent's boat and grabbed the old man's right hand. That's when he lost it.

He sobbed great, loud sounds that did nothing to ease the tremendous amount of pain he felt. It only increased when he got onto his knees and looked up at Vincent's face, which was usually sun kissed with a friendly expression. The old man's eyes, still open and staring at nothing, looked distant. As Sam gripped Vincent's cold, purple hand, his own hand trembled, and he reached up to close Vincent's eyes.

Sam collapsed inside the boat near Vincent's feet. He closed his eyes with his head between his knees, wishing this moment was just a nightmare.

"I can't do this. I can't do this." He repeated the phrase over and over.

He slammed his fist on the wood floor of the boat in frustration, with his chest shaking as he struggled to breathe between fits of crying. As he laid inside Vincent's boat, every second brought an almost inconceivable hurt, one he had never felt before. Every breath was painful, as if his lungs didn't want to keep working. His limbs seemed heavy like he would never be able to move them, and his heart felt as if someone had crushed it and left it useless.

He kept his head between his knees and cried until he physically couldn't anymore. His breaths were so short and rapid he felt as if he would suffocate. He tried to slow his breathing and regain composure. Keeping his eyes closed, he cleared his mind as best he could. His breaths began to get deeper and longer. He finally calmed enough to regulate his breathing.

When he opened his eyes he had to shake the urge to look back at Vincent. If he didn't get up to call Chris he knew there'd be a search party forming soon. He took his phone out of his pocket and surprisingly had service—just one bar, enough to get him through to Chris.

"Hey, you found him?" Chris said upon answering.

Sam paused before speaking, hating to say the words.

"He's dead."

Seventeen

In the end, it wasn't the mighty Atchafalaya that claimed Vincent like Sam had feared. Instead, Vincent took with him a part of the Atchafalaya that would be lost forever. Vincent's memories and touch on the landscape of the Basin vanished in an instant, the moment he took his final breath and his heart thudded its last thud. No longer would Sam hear the old man's laugh echo through the cypress. No longer would Vincent's hands haul fish into his boat on a steamy morning on Riley Bayou. He wouldn't be there to tell stories late into the night about the good old days, the ones when Sam's parents also made their mark on the Basin.

Vincent succumbed to a heart attack while he was on the way to meet up with Sam, dying just a day after his 78th birthday.

The old Cajun's death didn't make the only newspapers in the nearby towns of Pierre Part or Plaquemine. Most of the locals didn't even know who the old man was. Sam had no way of notifying Vincent's brother Tony of the news, and other than Tony, Sam didn't know of anyone else he should contact about Vincent's passing. There wasn't a funeral or any public mourning period that followed. Those who wept for Vincent did it by themselves in private.

Sam peered out of the window of Chris' truck. He had paid little attention to his surroundings throughout the drive. They were leaving Baton Rouge, Louisiana's capital an hour and a half north of Bayou Pigeon, after picking up the old man's cremated remains. Sam struggled to focus on anything and seldom looked beyond the window of Chris' truck during the drive.

Sam had Vincent's remains encased in a large urn held between his legs on Chris' bench seat, destined for the only place he thought they should be: Riley Bayou. Vincent had always said he wanted his ashes to be sprinkled around the Atchafalaya, his home and the place he would always cherish. Sam wanted to scatter them into the water one morning, early enough to catch the steam rising from the bayous. It was the part of the day that reminded Sam the most of Vincent, and a time of day that Vincent loved.

Vincent always said mornings were so special because it was like a blank canvas, the whole day out ahead with every decision made shaping a part of the picture. It could be a good day or bad one, and ultimately that was up to each individual. He would say he liked to make his a "*bon matin*," a French phrase meaning "good morning," by starting with a cup of coffee. After that, the rest was easy, he said.

"You gonna want to do something with those ashes?" Chris asked. He drove slowly around the curvy bayou roads. "Gonna want to sprinkle them somewhere or keep them with you?"

Sam struggled to speak, but it wasn't due to tears, as much as from a reluctance to vocalize anything. He and Chris hadn't spoken much on the way to the capital city and the few words they shared as they got closer to their home near the Atchafalaya felt forced. He looked down at the urn. "I'd like to scatter them, but if you don't mind, I'd like to do it myself."

"I understand. He would want you to be the one who spread out his ashes."

Chris turned left down the road that paralleled the Atchafalaya levee not far from Vincent's home. "Sam, there's something I have for you."

Sam shifted his attention from the levee outside the window to Chris.

"Vincent left a will for you. He wrote it just a few weeks ago. I helped him with it, and he told me to give it to you if he should pass. I don't know why he chose to write it then, but he did. I'll give it to you when you're ready to look at it."

Sam looked back out the window, trying to contain the urge to cry. "That's fine," he mumbled lowly. He didn't want to read the will, yet. He knew all that would do was make the fact that Vincent was gone seem more real. And he didn't want to see what the old man intended to leave behind. Just the idea of reading the will pained him.

Chris kept his focus on driving and didn't press Sam to speak anymore until they had gotten to Vincent's house. The afternoon was cloudy and gray. Another cold front was making its way south, again plunging daytime temperatures down. The wind started to knock off many of the leaves on the trees surrounding the old house, giving it an eerie and dismal appearance under the pale light that managed to escape through the clouds.

"Look, man, if you need anything just give me a call. I'm here for you. If you need someone to talk to or anything, just let me know," Chris said, shifting his truck into park.

Sam began gathering his belongings from the floor-board of the truck. "I appreciate that, Chris. I'll be in touch with you soon. I just need some time."

"I understand. Whenever you're ready, give me a call."

"Thanks." Sam nodded to Chris as he stepped out of the truck. He walked up the stairs to the old house and through the door. He zipped up his jacket all the way to his neck to keep warm inside the old shack. He looked around at the inside at everything sitting exactly as Vincent had left it. The dented tin percolator sat on the antique stove to his left, near a single sink with a few cups in it. The flannel coat Vincent wore on his final day was draped over one of the kitchen chairs to Sam's right.

He set the urn down on the table and sat in the exact chair he had the day he met Vincent. He stared at the other chair, the one Vincent had often sat in across from him while they shared a cup of coffee or a story together. It was there that they enjoyed countless meals and cups of coffee over the last few months, and it was also where Sam disclosed feelings and emotions to the old man that he had never spoken about before. Vincent had a way of listening and a calming facial expression that eased Sam, enough so that he wanted to tell the old man everything. They had never hidden anything from one another.

Tears formed in Sam's eyes. It was still too soon to be inside the home. He walked outside, back into the windy evening to get some fresh air.

A light rain started pelting his face, so he walked to the backyard, under the roofed area where he had learned how to butcher fish. Almost as soon as he stepped under the cover of the tin roof, he knew being there was a mistake. He could see Vincent standing next to the stainless steel sink, explaining how to cut up a catfish or the best way to chop up frog legs. He placed his hand on one of the old man's filet knives, the one he had used when he cut his hand on the catfish. Usually, that memory caused him to laugh, but now all it did was remind him of what he had—what he had lost.

He turned his head and spotted on the grass the pirogue he had made. It sat upright, just like Vincent had left it a few nights before. He remembered how he and Vincent were supposed to take it out for the first time to hunt ducks at the mouth of the river. They were planning to use the pirogue as their mode of transportation to navigate the shallow marsh of the delta, which held a sizeable group of waterfowl.

Sam kneeled beside the pirogue and touched its side. He stood as a few tears fell onto the cypress boat. He remembered how Vincent told him how the houseboat had haunted him for years after Ryan and Martha died. When the old man would go back, he saw them everywhere. Sam, standing in the old man's backyard with tears rolling down his face, understood what Vincent meant. Everywhere he looked, he saw Vincent. The old man had said that after a while the feeling doesn't hurt as much, but Sam couldn't see how he would ever mend. His wounds, he thought, were beyond repair.

He briskly walked back into the house to grab the urn, then made his way back outside into the rain, sloshing through the muddy driveway to get into Vincent's old truck. He skidded down the path, taking a right onto the levee road toward the convenience store. He stopped at the gas station to buy a few days' worth of food, knowing he wouldn't have the energy or the desire to continue his daily routine of fishing and hunting.

When he walked in, Betsy, the same cashier that had greeted him when he was looking for Vincent, was working the register, her hair in disarray as it most always was. The two usually engaged in small talk, and Sam always enjoyed chatting with her, because she was a friendly person with a vibrant personality, and that day was no different.

"Hey, Sam, how's it going?" she said with a smile as she noticed him enter through the glass door.

"Going well," Sam said quietly with a forced smirk. He quickly walked down the small aisles to avoid further conversation and stuffed enough food to last for a week into a cracked, plastic basket. He returned to the front of the store and placed the items on the counter. Betsy scanned Sam's bags of potato chips, canned meat and granola bars.

"You stocking up or something?" she asked with a smile still on her face.

Sam gave another half-hearted smirk without responding. He looked beyond Betsy, at the shelf behind her. He stared at it, his eyes moving across its contents. He knew he shouldn't, and he knew it was wrong, but he asked anyway. "Can I get a fifth of that whiskey over there?" He pointed to a bottle sitting on the shelf behind Betsy.

"Sure, Sam," she said, noticing he wasn't in the mood for conversation.

He had asked hoping she'd say no. He hoped she would tell him it was a stupid idea and that drinking wouldn't solve anything—it would only lead to more hurt, more pain. Instead she walked to the shelf and grabbed the bottle, sliding it on the counter toward him.

"That'll be $32.50," she said after scanning the whiskey.

Sam paid and walked out, blank-faced, without saying goodbye or waiting for his change.

He drove Vincent's truck toward the boat landing, both hands gripping the steering wheel as he slouched over it slightly. He looked at the road, then at the plastic bags on the blue bench seat. The top of the bottle of whiskey poked out of one of them. He looked at it, with the urge to throw it out of the window, or shatter it against the dash, but instead he peered back at the road and continued driving.

He launched his boat into the water, parked Ole Blue, and then began the cold drive to Riley Bayou, making all the familiar turns past all the same scenery. The Atchafalaya didn't have the same effect on Sam as it normally did, as he zoomed past everything as fast as he could. He didn't bother to admire the beauty of the changing leaves or the packs of waterfowl flying high in the sky. His eyes barely focused on the bayou in front of him, as his conscious fought with his grief-stricken, confused mind, shouting at him for what he was about to do.

He got to his home, moored near the side of it and tied up the boat, walking onto his porch with the urn under one arm and the plastic bags in the other. When he got inside, he laid the urn and bags down on the floor, then sat in a chair near his table. He slid the whiskey on the table in front of him, and stared at it.

He sat without moving or breaking his stare at the bottle. Though he was within the confines of Riley Bayou and under the roof of his home, he still felt the pain. At this point, it made him feel physically ill. He wanted nothing more than to numb what he was feeling.

At that moment, Vincent's words of wisdom, which normally brought Sam solace, escaped him. The old man's hopeful thoughts floated just outside of reach. All that remained inside of Sam's head—and his heart—was hurt.

He knew it wasn't right, and he knew what opening the bottle meant. But he didn't care.

He reached across the table and grabbed it, twisted open the top, and slowly took a swig. His head tilted back as he closed his eyes. The sweet taste of the alcohol on his lips was familiar. The way it singed his throat as it made its way down to his stomach gave him chills.

He opened his eyes and quickly took another gulp—and then another. His thoughts became fewer after each swig. He welcomed the long forgotten, yet comfortable feeling of his blood buzzing through his veins. He loved the way it felt. He hated the fact that he did, but he loved it.

Before long, the bottle of whiskey was empty and Sam lay on the floor, so intoxicated he was barely conscious.

Eighteen

Sam came to just after sunset, lifting his head off the floor with a dizzying headache. Despite his pounding head, he wanted more alcohol.

He left the houseboat and made the trip back to the boat landing. Though not as belligerent as he had been just a few hours before, he was still drunk, with the mission of drinking until he couldn't drink anymore. A few hunters were loading their boats after an afternoon bagging a few ducks as Sam made it to the boat landing in the darkening sky. He barely managed to reverse Vincent's trailer into the water, almost jackknifing the vehicle during his attempts. He slogged around the launch, tying straps to secure the boat to the trailer. He fumbled over his feet and even fell once. The other boaters looked on in disgust.

When he finally loaded the boat on the trailer, he shot off to T's, a bar Chris had talked about on a few occasions. It was one of the only watering holes in the small village, frequented by locals after a day of fishing or hunting.

Sam managed to pull up to the ancient, cream-colored bar in one piece, parking Ole Blue near the rear of the gravel lot adjoining the building. Through the many windows of the front porch, Sam could see that the place was already harboring other fishermen as they rounded off a hard day of working in the Basin. Their pickup trucks lined the lot by the dozens and almost all had boats in tow.

He walked onto the weathered porch, past a few patrons who were drinking beer in the cold night, and shuffled through the red front door. The interior was dim with only a few low-hanging lamps spaced apart on the ceiling. Cajun zydeco music played softly through a jukebox in the corner of the room. On the white walls hung many black and white photographs of locals posing with alligators or deer with sizeable racks. Some just showed off the sheer volume of fish a few Cajuns had caught.

Sam spotted near the rear of the room the bar, constructed of unpainted plywood with only room for five stools. He stumbled that way, doing his best to dodge the tables that dotted the floor leading to it. Three men, donned in camouflage, lined the bar, but most sat at the tables topped with pitchers of beer. Sam sat at a stool near the edge of the bar, away from the nearest person.

The bartender, an older man with long hair styled in a ponytail, walked over to take Sam's order. He had round cheeks but a thin frame, hidden under a black vest. "What you having?" he said to Sam with a deep Cajun drawl.

"I want some whiskey, neat," he said to the bartender without looking up.

The bartender pointed to the bottles behind him. "We've got multiple kinds. Which one you want?"

Sam pointed to one of the options without looking. The bartender filled up a glass halfway and handed it over.

"That's $5," the man said.

Sam stuck a $20 bill onto the counter. "Here and give me three more."

The bartender took Sam's money and walked away to grab the bottle. Sam quickly gulped down the glass and held the cup over the edge of the bar for his refill. The bartender poured again and Sam took another gulp.

"You might want to slow down. It's early and you got all night."

"Just pour me another drink," Sam mumbled back.

The bartender filled the glass again, this time all the way to the top. "Here, that amounts to three." He walked away, visibly irritated.

Sam sat back and closed his eyes. He stayed at the bar for a half hour, sipping on the remainder of his whiskey. He thought his memories of Vincent would fade the more he drank, but with each sip, and with every minute that he became more inebriated, he felt worse, while the images of Vincent's lifeless body, and the anguish he felt, never dissipated.

When he finished the glass, he got up from the stool. He saw double, and despite the chilly temperatures inside the bar, he was sweating. At that point, all he wanted to do was sleep in his bed and be comforted by Riley Bayou. He walked toward the door with the intent on driving back to the swamp for the night. He only made it a few more steps before he stumbled. He fell onto a table, grabbing a nearby chair to halt his downward trajectory. An empty pitcher tumbled off the table and to the floor. Sam sat down, ran his fingers through his hair, and tried to gain some composure.

All the noise claimed the attention of a few people near him. A number of them looked over, laughed, and went about their loud conversations. But one kept looking. He stood and walked to the table where Sam sat.

"Well, it's the son of a bitch who thought he could whoop my ass with a piece of wood."

Sam looked up with his eyes barely open. Though the room was spinning, he knew exactly who stood in front of him. It was the gun-wielding man that broke into the house-boat a few months ago.

"You a little drunk or something?" the man asked.

Sam looked up, head swaying from side to side, eyes still barely open, and said with a sarcastic tone, "Or something."

"You a smart ass, too, huh?"

"Leave me alone. I'm not trying to get into anything."

"You must like telling me what to do," the man said as he leaned toward Sam. "I'll do whatever the hell I want."

"I'm not looking for trouble."

"He's not looking for trouble," the man said to his two friends at a nearby table as he laughed. He leaned over on the table and got closer to Sam's face and shouted, "Come on. Get up! Get out that damn chair and get outside. We gonna settle what we didn't finish."

Sam held up his hand and shook his head. "Look, I said I don't want any trouble."

"I don't give a damn what you said!" the man shouted, picking up a chair near Sam and slamming it onto the ground.

The bartender overheard the noise and intervened. "Y'all take that outside, Will, I don't want any of this in here tonight," he said from behind the bar.

Will looked up at the bartender with a smile. "Of course." He snarled then punched Sam in the temple. Sam plummeted out of the chair to the floor face first and winced in pain. Before he could get up, Will grabbed him by his jacket's hood and started dragging him outside, followed by two others. Will opened the door and threw Sam forward onto the cement.

"Get up! Come on!" Will shouted.

Sam struggled to his feet, holding his head and reeling from the blow he had just taken. He knew there would be no way of talking his way out of the situation. So, with his head still swaying from side to side, he picked up his fists and got ready to give the man what little he had left.

"Come on then, damn it! I'm standing right here," Sam shouted back. He could barely see Will standing in front of him, his vision was blurred just like the rest of his senses.

Will smiled and approached Sam. He confidently reared back and swung, but Sam ducked just in time. Will, who appeared almost as drunk as Sam, stumbled after missing his mark.

Sam recovered from dodging the blow and, with Will knocked off balance, hit Will firmly in the stomach.

Will staggered backward and held his mid-section, the blow having knocked the wind out of him. Noticing a window of opportunity, Sam lunged forward and tackled him. The two men wrestled around on the porch of the bar as Will's friends stood close by.

Sam forced his way on top of Will. It was all too much: the grief from Vincent's death, along with the frustration of resorting to alcohol, and the buildup of horrifying memories from his childhood that always plagued him. It sent all of his feelings rushing to the surface, and he screamed as if they had all banded together and escaped at that very moment.

Sam punched Will right in the chin, his sloppy blow barely connecting. He reared back for the second one, hitting

Will's mouth. His strength surged, fueled by his raging emotions. He punched again, this one solid and splitting Will's upper lip. As he reared back again for a fourth, he felt a blow to the back of his head and he collapsed on top of Will. His ears rang, and his energy abandoned him.

Will shoved Sam off him and stood up woozily, wiping blood from his face. "Why'd you do that, damn it?" Will said to his friend, who held a shattered beer bottle. "I was about to get up and finish him. You son of a bitch." He focused back on Sam.

The combination of the alcohol and the recent blow made the night dizzying, and all Sam could see was a blur. He forgot where he was, but he didn't forget the hurt. For a second, he thought he saw Vincent in the distance, puffing on a cigarette. He reached his hand up into the air and tried to call out to him. He wanted to say he was sorry. He wanted the old man to hug him and bring him back to Riley Bayou, and tell him a story about his mom and dad, just like they used to do, but instead the image disappeared.

Will walked over to Sam and crouched down on one knee. He picked up Sam by the jacket. "I ain't never seen you around here," he said as blood still streamed down his lip, "and I don't know who the hell you are, but I know I don't like you. I better not ever see you in here again. And here's to make sure you never forget that."

Will shoved Sam's head into the cement. He then began punching him as hard as he could.

Sam absorbed blows to his eyes, his nose, and his chin, as each hit covered his face with more blood. He didn't feel anything anymore. He couldn't move. He tried to search for the image of Vincent again, though he couldn't muster anything but darkness. He lay on the parking lot outside of T's, unable to fight back.

Nineteen

Sam awoke, lying in a hospital bed in a cluttered room in the Pierre Part Clinic. The white lights of the hallway just outside the door were blocked by the curtain surrounding him. The dimly lit space was only big enough for the bed and a couch.

Initially, Sam struggled to make sense of where he was. He felt dazed, sluggish, as if he were stuck between reality and a dream. He slowly opened one eye and then the other, his vision terribly blurred, before he fell back into a state of drowsiness.

Moments later he opened his eyes again. This time, his mind began to clear, and he gathered what little strength he had to attempt to lift his head. He turned and saw Chris sleeping on the couch and hoarsely called for him.

Chris jumped up and walked near the bed, touching Sam's shoulder. "Hey, man, you awake? You doing alright?"

Sam waited a few moments to respond. "I...I think so."

"That's good to hear. Man, you sure look like hell."

Sam squinted his eyes, which were still swollen and badly bruised. He had five stitches in his right cheek, just under where the purple color faded from his eye socket.

Bandages covered a gash on his chin and a brace bounded his broken nose. He touched a large bandage around his head, which covered the wound from the beer bottle shattering across his skull. "How'd I get here?"

"After you got the life beat out of you, I just so happened to show up at the right time to knock Will off of you and brought you here. The doctor said a few more punches in the right place and you could've suffered some serious damage."

"What time is it?"

"It's almost noon. You been out for a solid two days almost. You've got a concussion. Luckily there's no brain damage or anything."

Sam shifted his body up in the hospital bed so that he could sit. Even with the pain medication, his head pounded with every small movement. "That guy, he was the one that tried to break into my houseboat," he winced, getting into a comfortable sitting position.

Chris sat down on the sofa and leaned over with his elbows on his knees. "So that's how he knows you."

"He just came up to me and wanted to fight out of nowhere."

"He's a no good piece of trash. I called the cops and told them what happened after I drove you over here. My cop buddy Ricky called me a little while later that night and said they booked Will for assault on a police officer and resisting arrest. Turns out he put up a little fight when they got there. That'll be in addition to what he did to you. They also booked his friend for aggravated battery for knocking you in the head. And they got plenty of eyewitnesses. Hopefully he goes away for a while now. Ain't his first time in jail."

Sam rubbed his fingers along the stitches on his face. "I feel terrible."

"You look even worse. I'm surprised you even remember anything. The doc said you might have temporary memory loss when you woke up."

"For the most part I think I remember everything before I blacked out." He wished he didn't. Consciousness brought back memories of Vincent, finding him lifeless, his eyes vacant.

The pain of that day started to stab him again.

"That's a good sign." Chris paused for a moment. "Look, I know you're probably still delirious from everything, but you know he wouldn't want this, Sam. He wouldn't want you to act like this, you know that."

"I told you I didn't do anything to provoke the guy. He just came after me."

"The bartender told Ricky that you were so drunk you could barely stand."

"And?" Sam looked away from Chris, too embarrassed to own up to what he'd done. His frustration at himself for drinking almost outweighed his grief at losing Vincent. While he regretted the way he acted, he didn't want to say so, as if by admitting what he'd done would make it more real.

"Sam, you can't bury his memory away with alcohol, trust me, it doesn't work."

"Yeah and how would you know?" What business was it of Chris' to tell him how to cope with the loss of Vincent? Chris didn't know what he'd been through.

Chris paused with an uncomfortable expression on his face, and cleared his throat. "I never talk about Iraq. Not because I don't have a lot to talk about, but because it was one of the most horrible times of my life. I lost five friends in the two years I was there. One of them was my best friend. His name was Marcus Rogers. He got blown up by an IED about fifty yards in front of me one morning while we were on patrol. I watched his body separate right in front of my eyes."

Chris looked down at the floor and shook his head, struggling to continue. He looked back to Sam. "It's been ten years since then, and there's not a day that goes by that I don't think about that. That I don't think about the horror I saw while I was out there. There's not a night that goes by that I don't wake up in sweats. No matter how much I drink, the pain doesn't go away. No matter how much whiskey I shove down my throat, it doesn't change the fact that everything happened the way it did. All it does is numb everything temporarily. I can't change that, but I know you are more than that. Vin wouldn't want to see you act like that because of him."

Sam stared at the wall and fought to keep tears from rolling down his face. "Chris, I'm sorry. I didn't know. Vin never told me anything about that."

"Vin didn't know about that. No one does."

"It just hurts so bad. I don't want to feel this way anymore. I don't know what else to do." Sam's words trailed off as he began to sob.

Chris came to the bed and put his hand on Sam's. "Look, I know coming from me, this may seem hypocritical, but it sure ain't at the bottom of a bottle. If anything, it's time. It'll be tough for a while—for maybe even a long time. But after a while, it'll get better."

Sam wiped tears from his eyes and looked up at Chris

with a worried look, his forehead wrinkled and his lip quivering. "And if it doesn't?"

"It will. You can't think like that."

"But it hasn't gotten better for you."

"In some ways it has. When I first got back stateside I didn't sleep at all. I was a mess. I can't say I'm healed or ever will be, but time has helped. This for you will pass, Sam, I know it will."

Sam exhaled loudly. "I hope so." He tensed his muscles, clenching his hands before he continued. "When I was a kid, before I went to bed at night, I'd pray. To who or what, I don't even know. But I asked that I could just spend one day with my parents. Just one. I only wanted to see them, touch them. If I couldn't have a family, I at least wanted to know what it felt like to be a part of one for a day."

Sam quelled his urge to start sobbing again, as he fought to continue to speak. "I finally was at a point in my life where everything made sense. I actually had a sense of family. I had things to look forward to, and I had something in my life that had been missing since my childhood. Then in an instant it's gone. And in the process I lost a man that was the closest thing to a father I'll ever have."

"Sam, you still have things to look forward to in life. Just because he's gone doesn't mean your life is hopeless. You still have the life you've been building here."

"It doesn't? Because I'm pretty sure once again I'm alone in this world. Maybe it's just the way I'm supposed to live my life: alone and in disarray. It's the only thing I know."

Sam again looked away from Chris. This burst of self-pity wasn't like him, and he hated feeling the way he did. But at that point, everything was too much for him to feel strong.

He couldn't accept Vincent's death, and it felt like his world had crashed down on him and would never be mended.

Chris walked over to a jacket he had draped on a chair. He reached inside the pocket and returned to Sam. "I wouldn't give you this if I didn't know what it said. I didn't know what it was so I read through some of it yesterday. I stopped a bit through to give you some privacy. It was mixed in with Vincent's will. I think you need to read it. I think it'll help you see what I can't say myself."

Chris handed Sam a folded piece of paper. Sam took it and unfolded it. It was a hand-written note from Vincent. It read:

> Sam,
>
> If you're reading this, it means I've left the world for good. No matter what, I don't want you to be sad at all. I lived a hell of a life, one that was long and full of happiness. You a strong person and I know you'll get along fine without me because the moment I met you, I knew you were a tough one. Strong and determined.
>
> The end of my life before you came along was lonely. Just because I put on a smile everyday doesn't mean everyday was easy. About six months before you showed up I went to the doctor, and he told me I would be lucky to live another year with all the smoking and the way I ate. I had all kinds of blockage in my heart. And he didn't think I'd make it through surgery because of what

bad shape my heart was in. He said having a heart attack was a question of when, not if. I had lost all hope before you came along, and I was just waiting for the day to come when I would stop breathing. I once thought I would never get the chance to see you again, even though not a day went by that I didn't think of you. When you came along I knew it was fate. It was the way it was supposed to be. My life changed like I never thought it could at my old age. Every day was special, spending time with you. I know you probably see it as I helped to change your life, but I can say you changed mine just as much.

You such a special young man. You remind me so much of your parents. Like I always said, you have the best of both of them in you, and that's all you'll need in life. Just remember to live life the way you have been and you'll be just fine.

I love you, Sam, like a son that I never had. I loved your parents like they were my children, too. I have regretted every day of my life that I didn't fight harder to keep you when you were young. It's a decision that has plagued me for all of these years. I tried my best to make up for that. I hope I've done good. One thing I know is that I've been blessed to have known Ryan, Martha, and you. Your family was the best thing that I had in my life. You three will always hold a special place in my heart, in this life and the next.

If there's one thing I want you to know, it's that your talents and hard work will take you far in this life. I know you destined for more than living out your life as a fisherman. I saw that from the first day you came to live here. You so smart. Use that, Sam. Don't think you need to sell yourself short. You a fast learner just like your father. That kind of talent isn't in everybody.

Always remember: *famille, amour, une vie.*

Sincerely,
Vincent Dupuis

Sam's hand trembled as he held the note. As he finished reading, he folded the paper and closed his eyes. Vincent's words rung throughout his head, and instead of tears, they started to bring him an unexpected bout of clarity in him. He sat in silence for a spell, replaying the words from his best friend over through his head. "He knew all along he didn't have much longer," he finally said as his eyes opened.

"I'm still shocked about that."

"I came along right before he thought he was about to die. If I would've came to Louisiana just a little later none of this would have been possible. Why didn't he tell me?"

"Maybe he didn't want you to view him differently. He probably knew if he told you that everything would've been different. He knew we would treat him like an old sick man."

Sam nodded in agreement. "Yeah, I guess you're right."

He reflected on the note, about the bar fight, drinking the alcohol. He breathed deep as Vincent's words filled him with the courage to continue. "Thank you, Chris. I needed to read that. I'm sorry for putting you through this." He lowered his head in embarrassment.

"Hey, man, don't apologize. I'm just glad I came along when I did. If I wouldn't have, you might not be sitting here right now. You'd probably be lying face first in a ditch."

"You're right, this isn't me, and he wouldn't have wanted me to act like that. I'm ashamed of what happened."

"You're going through a rough time. Like I said, it'll pass, Sam."

Sam looked at Chris and smiled, despite his swollen lips. "Vin was right; you really are a good friend to have. Thanks for everything."

Chris smiled back. "You're welcome. I'll always be here for you when you need help. But you've got a good head on your shoulders. I figure I won't need to be rescuing you from any more bar fights."

* * *

Chris picked Sam up from the health clinic, and they went straight to the Atchafalaya. Only three days after the fight, and with strict rules on what he could do for the next few weeks, the only thing Sam wanted was to be back in Riley Bayou.

On the boat ride in, Sam sat in the front of Chris' skiff and soaked in the Atchafalaya's beauty, much like he did that day he witnessed the wilderness for the first time. Though now, Sam noticed how different the place he called home looked than it had just a few months prior. The Atchafalaya during the summer was a seemingly endless jumble of green-ery, the result of sub-tropical temperatures promoting vege-tation growth on every tree, overturned log, and patch of dirt that wasn't underwater. Sam hadn't really noticed the trans-formation to fall and winter taking shape before Vincent's death. His routine and continued stays within the Basin meant the incremental changes were hardly noticeable. His brief stay away from the wilderness combined with his slow, methodical studying of his surroundings expounded all of the subtle variances around him. He looked up at the cypress trees, their branches now mostly bare as many of the needle-like leaves had fallen. The lack of leaves meant much of the forest had a brown tinge to it, but visible in spurts were signs of life, if he only looked hard enough to see them. Blooming flowers, colored red and yellow, covered the forest floor while, every now and then, a cluster of green foliage still clung to life on a tree. He breathed deeply and the sweet aroma unique to the Basin, accentuated with pollen from the blooming flowers, filled his lungs.

Chris made the turn through the cypress trees and into Riley Bayou a few hours before the sun would set for the day. He moored near the houseboat's porch and helped Sam get out of the skiff. "You got it?" he said, grasping Sam's elbow to offer stability.

"Yeah, thanks." Sam moved slowly to climb up to the porch.

"You should have enough food to last you until the weekend. I dropped off a bunch yesterday. I'll come by every day or so to make sure you're doing OK."

"I appreciate that Chris. I'll be fine though, really."

Chris, standing at the rear of his boat, looked down the bayou. Yellowed leaves spiraled from nearby trees and danced in the air before landing on top of the water. "He'll always be here with you," Chris said as he continued to gaze at the swamp.

Sam turned to look at the bayou. A slight gust of wind brushed across his face, and his hair fluttered lightly. He smiled. "That's what makes this place so special."

Epilogue

It was a little more than a year after Vincent's death, and Sam was still getting accustomed to living back on dry land, let alone running a business. It still didn't feel real to him, the fact that he was selling pirogues and paintings for a living, not to mention that he set up shop in Breaux Bridge, his mother's home town. The small, tin building, which was positioned in front of the modest home he bought just a month prior, was still pretty bare. He had a few pirogues spaced here and there, as well as some of his paintings adorning the walls, but for the most part, he had a lot of space to fill.

Sam scurried around, hoping to close earlier than normal. He was preparing to leave for Riley Bayou and the houseboat for the afternoon, which was about an hour drive from his new home, and much farther from Bayou Pigeon where Vincent once lived. The front door opened while he was bent down behind a counter putting a few tools away. He looked up to see an elegant young woman, with vibrant brown hair curling to her lower back. After giving her a simple glance, Sam thought that everything about her was charming, from her modest white dress stained with paint to the fact that she was barefoot.

Sam watched her as she looked around the inside of the space. She made eye contact with him, and his gut instantly churned with nervousness. Realizing he was staring, he said with a shaky voice, "Can I help you?"

"I'm just here to look around," she said in a soft, Cajun tone. "I heard from a friend there was a new boutique open in town. Are you the owner?"

Sam shook his head. "I sure am. I'm Sam Landry."

"I'm Elise. It's nice to meet you." She walked up to Sam and shook his hand. Her dainty, soft hand was engulfed in Sam's, which were specked with old splinter wounds and dotted with paint.

"You're really good," she said, motioning to a painting that hung on the wall nearby.

Sam looked at the work she pointed to and smiled. It was a portrait of Vincent, and one of his favorites. The old man was pictured in his overalls, without a shirt, and he had a cigarette positioned loosely in his mouth. But Sam still somehow managed to capture the old man's infectious smile through his weathered, gray beard.

"Thanks."

"These are all good, really. I love your sunrise painting here with the cypress trees. It's almost like I'm there, watching it. Your use of color is brilliant. You'll have to show me how you made this red."

"Are you an artist, as well?"

Elise picked up the bottom of her paint-stained dress and shook it lightly. "How'd you guess?" She laughed softly. "I live just up the road. I sell my work at the farmer's and arts market on Saturdays. You should come by sometime."

"Didn't know they had one here. I'll have to check that out soon."

Elise walked around the right side of the building, her hand gliding on a pirogue that rested on a countertop.

Sam stood behind the counter, watching her every move, as if he was in a trance. He figured she couldn't be older than her early twenties. Her petite figure swayed as she walked, exuding elegance as she gently gazed at Sam's artwork.

"And you sell these pirogues, too?" she asked.

"Sure do. I make them right out back. Well, that one you're looking at was made at my old home in the Basin."

"You used to live in the Atchafalaya?" her eyes widened with curiosity and she walked over to the counter. "I love going out into the swamp. For how long were you there?"

"About a year. I lived there with a close friend for a little while. Fished to make a living before I started painting and making the pirogues. And before that I lived in Boston."

"Sounds like you might have quite the stories with all the places you've been. I'd love to hear about that sometime."

"Anytime. I'm sure I've got more stories than you would ever want to hear."

Elise laughed softly and looked at Sam.

She was close enough now that he could see her eyes, which were a hazel color that took him back a year to the first time he saw Vincent. He looked at her and could see the same compassion and warmth he had grasped from Vincent's eyes. Sam thought there was something about her and the way she looked at him, that made him feel something he hadn't felt since Vincent was alive. He got lost in his thoughts before realizing he was staring too long. His face reddened and he turned around.

"Here, let me give you a card. I know I have some around here somewhere."

Sam kneeled near the counter and fumbled with paper and folders.

Elise let out a giggle. "I know where to find you," she said, making her way to the door. "Plus, I'll be seeing you around at the farmer's market, remember?"

Sam stood and said with a laugh, "That's right. I'll be sure to come by this weekend."

"Nice talking with you, Sam Landry."

"You, as well."

Sam walked up to the front window to watch as Elise walked back outside and got on her bike. He smiled as she peddled hard across the road to an adjacent gravel path. He stood there near the door, still filled with exuberance and a tad of nervousness. He walked over to a calendar he kept on the wall near the register, circled the upcoming Saturday with a black marker, and jotted an 'E' on the date.

Sam finished up closing the shop and walked outside and fired up Ole Blue, Vincent's aged pickup. The truck still ran remarkably well; of course Sam had installed a new transmission a few months ago.

Sam guided the old truck off the pavement onto a gravel road that led to the boat launch just outside of Breaux Bridge, nearly 20 miles on the other side of the Basin from where he used to launch near Bayou Pigeon. The sun glowed bright and barely a cloud hung in sight. It was early spring, one of Sam's favorite times to be in the Atchafalaya, mostly

due to the abundance of blooming flowers. As soon as he
started to guide his boat into the interior of the swamp, he
spotted deep hues of yellow, red, purple, and white that covered the forest floor and climbed up to the tree tops.

Almost an hour boat ride later and Sam arrived in Riley
Bayou.

He moored his skiff in the usual spot near the front
porch and walked inside. He hadn't had the time to frequent
his old home lately, so he looked around the place with a
nostalgic gleam in his eyes. It hadn't changed. It was still simple with the same charm that captured him the first day he'd
stepped in. He walked over to a shelf in the corner of the
room and picked up Vincent's urn.

He went back outside and strolled down the walkway
hovering above the water on the side of the houseboat. The
pirogue he built Vincent sat upside down near the edge of
the once sagging part of the home. He gently moved the boat
upright, took it off the porch, and slid it into the stained,
black water.

Sam scooted into the pirogue with care, and it sunk
down into the water, bobbing slightly with the added weight.
He set the urn in the middle of the pirogue near his feet. He
used a hand-crafted paddle to travel north up the bayou, and
looked around at the area he had lived in isolation for a little
more than a year with a deep, observant stare. The scene
down Riley Bayou was almost always different and that day
was no exception. It was a quality that Sam had grown to
love about the slice of swamp. White azaleas covered the
edge of the bayou like a runway lit up with lights at night. He
breathed deeply of their aroma that was so sweet he could
taste them.

At a spot where he used to set trotlines, and the houseboat no longer in view, he stopped paddling. The area had a cypress tree, greater in size than any others around. It had been spared years ago by the loggers that harvested much of the virgin cypress forest that once covered the Atchafalaya. It wasn't straight like the others around it at that time long ago, and it was hollow, so it was deemed unfit for lumber.

The giant tree, probably more than five hundred years old, rose higher than all of the younger trees in the vicinity, like a father guarding his family. It was crooked and deformed, but still majestic, mainly due to its size. Even the cypress knees, the roots that surrounded the tree, were taller than Sam. Cypress was the one feature of the landscape that reminded him most of everything in Louisiana: the Atchafalaya, his parents, Vincent, and the new life he had created there.

He knew it was the perfect place to spread Vincent's ashes.

Sam opened the top of the urn and he began gently sprinkling. The gray ashes poured out and mixed in the murky water, slowly dissipating after floating a few moments, until he couldn't see them anymore. He paddled up to the tree, through the ring of cypress knees, and tossed the rest at its base. He put his hand to the tree and closed his eyes. Through the rough exterior of the tree, he felt the old man's presence.

Releasing Vincent's ashes was the final gesture that would complete the closure Sam needed. It was a long journey to get to where he was in his life, a place where he could finally accept that Vincent was gone.

The last year had been tough, brutal at times. Yet some

days, Sam would be comforted by the warm words Vincent had written in his goodbye letter, while on other days being in the Atchafalaya, surrounded by memories of Vincent, hurt him. The hard days made him question if being in Louisiana was right for him.

He took a deep breath, pulling the atmosphere of the Basin into his lungs, thankful he hadn't let himself run away. The place captured him like nothing else ever before in his life: the smells, the immense beauty, and the wildness of it. The epicenter of that draw was in Riley Bayou, the place he felt most at home.

Sam realized that the pain from losing Vincent would never completely subside. Rather, he would have to learn to live with it—to press on despite it. Time wouldn't make Vincent's death disappear. It would remain a part of his life until he, too, took his last breath. This revelation didn't happen suddenly, but was rather an understanding that he developed through living a solitary life. The wilderness that had worked to help him confront the issues he grappled with throughout much of his life also aided in his acceptance of Vincent's death. Eventually, he saw the Atchafalaya as a place where he knew he could always see the old man if he looked hard enough. While at first he was haunted by the images of Vincent, he learned to welcome them, as a way to see the man who helped change his life.

He knew his search for family, for a sense of belonging, didn't end with Vincent's death. He was still on that path. If anything, he knew, more than ever, exactly what he was looking for.

Sam nodded his head, a symbolic farewell to Vincent, before paddling away from the cypress. He looked up to the trees that hung over the bayou and closed his eyes. He breathed in the moist, swamp air and opened his eyes as he exhaled. He smiled because he knew he wasn't alone. Ryan, Martha, and Vincent were always with him, wherever he went.

Author's Note

THE ATCHAFALAYA RIVER BASIN, the last bastion of wilderness in Louisiana, spans roughly 1 million acres, and is the largest wetland in the United States. Its cypress-tupelo swamps and grassy marshes teem with creatures like alligators, garfish, venomous snakes, and black bears. Its landscape is formidable, yet visually stunning, where the only highways are bayous, and cathedrals come in the form of old-growth cypress trees.

Beginning in the mid 18th century, the Acadian people of Acadia (present day Nova Scotia), were exiled by the British. Many of them relocated to the swampland of the Atchafalaya Basin. In their new home, these Acadians, a term later shortened to Cajuns, braved hurricanes, weathered devastating floods and survived the torment of heat and mosquitoes. Their culture, in turn, is tough, but a proud, vibrant one that thrived—and still does today. Their food, songs, and way of life are connected to the land that provided for them so much so that it's now inseparable.

In an effort to protect Baton Rouge and New Orleans from flooding along the Mississippi River, in the mid-20th century, the Atchafalaya Basin was engineered into a spillway to act as an overflow container to fill up with water and relieve pressure on the Mississippi River when it got too high. Levees were constructed around the wilderness, creating a long, skinny ring of earthen walls spanning across south Louisiana, while flood gates and control structures were built at the head of the Atchafalaya River, a distributary of the Mississippi. The seasonal floods inside the ring of levees became increasingly worse, and when the flood gates were opened, water levels reached devastating heights. Only twice—in 1973 and 2011—were the flood gates to the Atchafalaya Basin opened, which unleashed a monumental flood throughout the area that disrupted life for the people still living there.

These days, most Cajuns live outside the Atchafalaya's levees to escape the danger of flooding—and to enjoy modern conveniences like electricity and running water. But many still spend most of their days inside the Atchafalaya Basin, making a living catching crawfish, alligators, and fish, just like their ancestors did for hundreds of years before them. For a select few, those hardy enough to battle the elements, or perhaps those looking for their own slice of heaven, they call the Atchafalaya Basin home. They spend their lives between the levees.

Made in the USA
Charleston, SC
24 July 2016